DOMINION

An Apocalyptic Epic in Seven Books

BOOK II
PHOENIX

by

Compasse

Sacrata Dei Press
A Division of The Compasse Corporation

Front Cover Art: *Vanishing Dawn*, by Ben Hamrick

Back Cover Art: *Paradise Lost 1*, by Gustave Doré

Printed in the United States of America

For John Karol Mary, Jacinta Christopher, Gianna Anthony,
& David Guadalupe;

I pray that I may one day see the marvelous vision that you now
embrace...

Author's Note

What is Truth?

This question was posed by a Procurator from the Roman Empire nearly two thousand years ago. The irony of the inquiry is not lost on many, considering to Whom he directs his query.

In the Author's Note from *Seed*, I expressed my dismay that so many in our world no longer seemed to be asking the "big questions" of existence. What could be the cause of this apparent disinterest? A general apathy? A self-absorbed presumption? An outright fear of the possible answers? No matter the origin, I do not believe this avoidant indifference to be a good thing, and though I may not go as far as Socrates ("an unexamined life is not worth living"), I *do* believe humanity loses out when its members act not upon convictions based in solid reason, but *react* to concepts and circumstances based on their own misconceptions, tainted appetites, and inner turmoil.

So then, here I choose to begin at the beginning. Even before the point "Is there a God?" stands the question: is there such a thing as objective truth? Upon this question all the other great questions hinge—for if all is subjective and can be relegated to the preference and/or opinion of each person, then nothing can be known, and seeking answers to *any* question is little more than an exercise in futility.

But good reason, as well as our experience of existence, indicates that objective truth *does* exist. The laws of nature and the laws of mathematics, for instance, do not change from person to person; the acceleration rate of a falling body absent air resistance will always be 9.8 m/s², two plus two will always equal four, and (in keeping with our theme) even music has "laws" which can be experienced, such as certain notes striking a dissonance when played together.

This then being granted, is it possible that objective truth extends to other realms and disciplines? Somewhere along the line we seem to have limited our ability to declare the truth of a thing to only that which can be measured by the instruments of natural science. Yet this is not a very "reasoned" approach to measuring/observing things outside of this discipline. Matters of philosophy, theology, and even thought will never be "discovered" under a microscope. Our powers of creativity and reason are much too great to be limited in this manner.

Philosophy (the "love of wisdom") provides a different set of instruments for determining truth within its sphere. It can quickly identify false premises and contradictions (non-truths) in a proposition or argument. For instance, in today's growingly relativistic society, one might attempt to say, "You believe in a god who created everything—that is *your* truth. I believe there is no god and only random chance—that is *my* truth." The reality is, both of these statements cannot be true.

This deeper understanding of the nature of truth has tremendous implications because we naturally act based of what we believe. If our belief, for instance, is that a particular map is accurate, we will make certain turns and exits to get from Philadelphia to Phoenix. If the map *is* indeed accurate (objectively true), we will reach our destination. However, if we are using a faulty map, even our "reasonable" decisions to turn, exit, etc. will most likely *not* get us to our destination—despite our most sincere beliefs—because those beliefs hinge off a framework that is objectively flawed.

For those in the Christian Faith, "Truth" is more than a concept, it is a Person. Jesus Christ, the "Man-God", is proposed to be the full embodiment of "what is", and the antithesis of "what is not". So returning to our initial question, and without making specific claims here as to *which* beliefs are true and which are false, it is clear that there *is* an objective reality— whether humanly knowable or not—that does not change with personal opinion or public sentiments. The truth really *is* out there... and our pursuit of this reality may very well make all the difference.

– Compasse

...from **Seed**

An earthquake hits central Jerusalem as a young Muslim boy, Ibn Fatimah, witnesses the destruction of The Dome of the Rock, Islam's central shrine and ancient location of the Jewish Temple.

Clear across the globe, Marisha, the teenage daughter of reputed organized crime figure Alexandre Nesterov, runs away to wed Jeffrey Chardin against her father's wishes. Following their wedding, Marisha learns that her husband is part of a pagan cult led by a darkened presence who calls himself Luther. Having forced himself upon her, Luther delights in Marisha's conception of twins, Tobias Isaac (son of Jeffrey), and Jesse (son of Luther). The sense of liberation that Luther experiences from this moment is consummate, and his serial trysts of sensual pleasures parallels his ascending status within his own dark faith tradition.

The suicidal Marisha falls into despair as she learns of her pregnancy, knowing intuitively of Luther's paternity. Yet before she is able to follow through with her act of desperation, a seed of hope literally presents itself, and in a symbolic act of resolution, Marisha plants the seed with a promise to her unborn child(ren), that for their sakes, she would persevere.

As the time for delivery approaches, and the differing paternity of the twins is made manifest, Marisha in inspired to reach out for her sister, Vanya, for relief in any form. Vanya vows to come to her aid, but a mysterious vision and its accompanying loss of time prevent her from responding to her sister's urgent appeal. Believing her sister too has abandoned her, Marisha dies in the difficult birth and is buried, unbeknownst to all in attendance, in close proximity to the young sapling which she herself had planted.

The delayed Vanya arrives on the scene, devastated and at a loss as to what to do; yet providence permits her to pose as a nanny to gain access to the two boys. Mysterious forces beyond her comprehension prevent her from fleeing with the twins, while a federal indictment renders her father powerless to assist her. Vanya solemnly accepts her virtual captivity for the sake of her nephews, serving especially as protector of Jesse, who is the object of abuse from both Jeffrey and Luther.

As years pass, their predicament intensifies, yet Vanya and the boys discover shelter from the maelstrom in music. As the abuse drives Jesse into deeper stages of withdrawal, Vanya rekindles the love of her younger years—playing different classical pieces on a harpsichord—serving as a beacon of solace which draws the young boy away from falling completely into the abyss of himself.

World events continue to present a deepening void, though unnoticed by the general population, which seems to be unconcerned about such matters. Following the assassination of *the Pope in Iraq, his successor, Christopher, experiences a moment of conversion at his election, provoking him to discard his initial agenda to "modernize" the Church. His detractors are successful in having him not only removed from office, but exiled and excommunicated. After months of the cardinals administrating the Church, one Leo XIV emerges at Pope, promoting the popularly desired agenda more sympathetic to the "modern world." Yet once again it would seem that providence intervenes when Leo's plane mysteriously disappears over the Atlantic Ocean, and he is presumed dead. A Roman cleric, who willingly participated in the ousting of Christopher, is elevated to the office of Pontiff, yet he too, following the path of Christopher, experiences a deep conversion and reasserts the traditional teaching of the Catholic Christian Church, much of which had been brought into question by Leo.*

Unbeknownst to Vanya, Luther moves forward in his plans to sacrifice his son, Jesse, in his sixth year; the final act in establishing himself as Grand Elder of what we now clearly see to be a global satanic assembly. The night before the ceremony, Jesse's brother, Tobias, learns of Luther's plans and manages to swap places with Jesse. Luther unknowingly sacrifices Tobias, as a devastated Vanya escapes with Jesse.

In the midst of the chaos, a mysterious figure slips into the Temple, placing his hand upon the slain Tobias in an apparent attempt to supernaturally resuscitate him. Yet a countering force enters from behind the figure, and the result of their confrontation remains unknown.

The book closes with Father Daniel Ananias, an American priest with Kurdish roots, miraculously surviving a nuclear dirty-bomb attack in Philadelphia.

PHOENIX

In the Garden of Paradise, beneath the Tree of Knowledge, bloomed a rose bush. Here, in the first rose, a bird was born. His flight was like the flashing of light, his plumage was beauteous, and his song ravishing. But when Eve plucked the fruit of the tree of knowledge of good and evil, when she and Adam were driven from Paradise, there fell from the flaming sword of the cherub a spark into the nest of the bird, which blazed up forthwith. The bird perished in the flames; but from the red egg in the nest there fluttered aloft a new one—the one solitary Phoenix bird. The fable tells that he dwells in Arabia, and that every hundred years, he burns himself to death in his nest; but each time a new Phoenix, the only one in the world, rises up from the red egg.

The bird flutters round us, swift as light, beauteous in color, charming in song. When a mother sits by her infant's cradle, he stands on the pillow, and, with his wings, forms a glory around the infant's head. He flies through the chamber of content, and brings sunshine into it, and the violets on the humble table smell doubly sweet.

But the Phoenix is not the bird of Arabia alone. He wings his way in the glimmer of the Northern Lights over the plains of Lapland, and hops among the yellow flowers in the short Greenland summer. Beneath the copper mountains of Fahlun, and England's coal mines, he flies, in the shape of a dusty moth, over the hymnbook that rests on the knees of the pious miner. On a lotus leaf he floats down the sacred waters of the Ganges, and the eye of the Hindoo maid gleams bright when she beholds him.

The Phoenix bird, dost thou not know him? The Bird of Paradise, the holy swan of song! On the car of Thespis he sat in the guise of a chattering raven, and flapped his black wings, smeared with the lees of wine; over the sounding harp of Iceland swept the swan's red beak; on Shakespeare's shoulder he sat in the guise of Odin's raven, and whispered in the poet's ear "Immortality!" and at the minstrels' feast he fluttered through the halls of the Wartburg.

The Phoenix bird, dost thou not know him? He sang to thee the Marseillaise, and thou kissedst the pen that fell from his wing; he came in the radiance of Paradise, and perchance thou didst turn away from him towards the sparrow who sat with tinsel on his wings.

The Bird of Paradise—renewed each century—born in flame, ending in flame! Thy picture, in a golden frame, hangs in the halls of the rich, but thou thyself often fliest around, lonely and disregarded, a myth—"The Phoenix of Arabia."

In Paradise, when thou wert born in the first rose, beneath the Tree of Knowledge, thou receivedst a kiss, and thy right name was given thee—thy name, Poetry.

— Hans Christian Andersen (1850)
The Phoenix Bird

1

Eyes I dare not meet in dreams
In death's dream kingdom
These do not appear:
There, the eyes are
Sunlight on a broken column
There, is a tree swinging
And voices are
In the wind's singing
More distant and more solemn
Than a fading star.

Let me be no nearer
In death's dream kingdom
Let me also wear
Such deliberate disguises
Rat's coat, crowskin, crossed staves
In a field
Behaving as the wind behaves
No nearer —

Not that final meeting
In the twilight kingdom.

– t.s. eliot
The Hollow Men

i

  Jonathan Storm navigated his Mustang Cobra IV convertible among the trash and potholes, slowly bringing his vehicle to a stop alongside the third house on Trinity Street. The security guard stood just inside the property line, and recognizing Jonathan he released the latch to pull the gate open.

"Good morning, Masias!"

The guard nodded in acknowledgment. "Good morning, Mr. Storm."

Jonathan tapped the horn lightly. A strong voice, which he instantly recognized as that of Mrs. Lindsey, rang out from inside the house.

"Nathan! Jonathan's here! Do you want to miss your graduation?"

A jovial voice shouted back, "Come on, Aunt Carol, you know they can't start the ceremony without the bottom of the class!"

Jonathan envisioned Mrs. Lindsey rolling her eyes and shaking her head, as she often had to do with Nathan's antics. Nathan was what one might call a "free spirit". His aunt and uncle, along with the rest of the civilized world, tried to tame him at every opportunity. To date, their efforts had been in vain.

Jonathan then heard the unmistakable sound of a guitar amplifier whining with feedback. He glanced upwards and saw his best friend, Nathan Page, standing atop the roof outside his window. Nathan held a guitar in his hands and sported nothing but his boxer shorts and graduation cap.

"Jon-boy!" he shouted down. "This one's for you!"

With his distortion pedal at its obvious maximum, Nathan struck a chord and began to sing at the top of his lungs:

> *"I'm at the top of my class*
> *Still my best friend's an ass*
> *Who's got this shit attitude.*
> *Yet one day I'll be great*
> *As a rich prick from Kent State*
> *While Nate panhandles for food!"*

Jonathan could do no more than shake his head. Again, the familiar sound of Mrs. Lindsey's scolding immediately followed.

"Nathaniel! You know I hate that language! Stop drawing attention to yourself—the neighbors are going to call the police!"

"Sorry, Aunt Carol," Nathan yelled back, chuckling. "The devil made me do it!"

Nathan winked at Jonathan and slipped back inside his window. The two were really quite a pair, Jonathan and Nathan, and no one could really figure out how they came to be—and even more amazingly *remain*—friends.

PHOENIX

They were an odd couple, no doubt. And despite Nathan's lyrics suggesting otherwise, Jonathan was actually graduating salutatorian. However, he felt it wise not to pick nits with this obvious oversight. Jonathan had always been an exceptional student, though he did manage to balance his studies with a personality endearing to all.

Nathan was another story altogether. Ever since the night he arrived with his aunt and uncle five years prior, trouble had seemed to follow just behind him. It was nothing serious, but if not better informed, one might have believed detention to be on Nathan's class schedule. He generally hung with a peer group quite un-affectionately referred to as the "neo-stones". Still, he and Jonathan often broke from their standard cliques to spend time together.

Jonathan could easily recall their first meeting, in a seventh grade philosophy class, where they found that their general perspectives on the "human condition" were about as far apart as could be. Still, they both enjoyed a good debate and had no trouble finding one when they were together.

"Hi ho, neighbor!"

Nathan emerged from the front door, zipping up his gown as he ran. He performed a cartwheel, perhaps to display the fact that he was only wearing his boxer shorts underneath, and hopped into the car.

Nathan offered Masias a feigned salute as they left. "Hold down the fort, Masias. Your prince shall return with a piece of paper that says I am superior to ninety-nine percent of the inhabitants of this God-forsaken world."

"Then I shall let you defeat me in the cribbage game this evening, Master Nathan."

"Nonsense!" Nathan called out. "There are some things—well, few things in this world—that must never change. That is one of them."

"Very well, sir."

Then, parading a larger-than-life grin on his face, Nathan turned to Jonathan. "Let's grab these diplomas before Waddock changes his mind!"

Jonathan smiled and began to back his car out, casually remarking, "Nate, my therapist is still waiting to hear from you..."

ii

"Yes, Mr. Nesterov, I thank you for your kindness. This… this is not something I would normally ask for… not something I would normally do."

"We live in difficult times, Mr. Petrall, which call for difficult choices to be made. Do not let a misguided sense of conscience dissuade you from doing what is best for your family."

The man looked down, still clearly not fully comfortable, but providing a slow nod of resolution. "Yes, thank you, Mr. Nesterov."

Alexandre Nesterov nodded to the man, then subsequently motioned to Mikhail Ostankino, who saw him out. Ostankino lit a cigarette as he returned to Nesterov's office and mechanically shut the double doors. Felix Amosov looked at the younger comrade with irritation as he absently shuffled through his pockets for a stick of nicotine gum. Both sat down in front of Nesterov's desk, appearing less than comfortable.

"Well?" Nesterov inquired.

The two men exchanged troubled glances. It was Amosov who broke the awkward silence.

"Still nothing, Alex."

Nesterov shook his head with an expression revealing a hint of despair. Unfortunately, he had grown used to this response. It had been the same answer every month for the last seven years, and it was not helping his position.

Danny Caputo, the man who Nesterov now answered to directly following the untimely demise of Vlad Ivankov, was to be executed in three days, having been convicted on seventeen counts of first degree murder and conspiracy to commit murder, along with a slew of other felonies. As the unlikely Russian right-hand man of the one time most feared mafia figures in the country, the responsibility of springing Caputo fell on the less-than-enthusiastic shoulders of Alexandre Nesterov.

It was Nesterov's obligation to threaten, bribe, or "terminate" whoever he had to in order to get Caputo out of his predicament. However, the opposing testimony had been so solid and the security so tight that following a botched bribe attempt to Senator William Maison, Nesterov found himself unable to even guarantee Caputo a pleasant last supper.

It was, indeed, a different world. The dirty bomb detonated in

PHOENIX

Philadelphia eleven years prior had set in motion dramatic actions and reactions which had transformed the political and cultural landscape of the country Nesterov had reluctantly come to call home. His dream of excusing himself from the syndicate had washed away as quickly as the collapse of the U.S. economy.

"Opportunity!" Caputo had called it. And indeed it was! Amidst the confusion, national shock, and desperation, organized crime was back in the golden days of post-Soviet Russia. It was all too easy, and in Nesterov's mind, necessary, to remain "in". Indeed, now it was clear that the ongoing safety of his family depended on it.

Yet, despite the many opportunities that availed their kind, Caputo was still to be taken down—a trophy used by higher-ups in the U.S. Government to prove that the tide was turning on the recent explosion in crime. In spite of all this, it was not the government that most concerned Nesterov at this time. He was loyal to a fault, and tried not to contemplate the mob wars which would take place if Caputo's sentence were not commuted. He knew that several syndicates ("families" was no longer an accurate term in the evolution of organized crime) from other parts of the country would vie for position. But even that was not actually the greatest of Nesterov's worries. Inheriting the full responsibility for the failure to get Caputo out, Nesterov would be a target for members from within his own association.

"So you are telling me," he began in a gruff voice, "that we do not even have a single lead on the whereabouts of Freeman or his family?"

"No, sir," Ostankino stated, sounding more meek than he would have preferred. He sucked in deeply on his cigarette, then looked down.

Harold Freeman had been the key witness in the trial against Caputo. A former small-time mob figure in Miami, Freeman had his résumé beefed up by the FBI and then infiltrated the Caputo organization as an undercover agent... even to the point of befriending Nesterov's son, Yerik. Five years later, Freeman was able to implicate Caputo and twenty-seven other members of the organization. Only by the grace of God were the charges against Nesterov thrown out. Though he used Freeman on some assignments by necessity, Nesterov had never trusted him and had avoided him like the plague.

"You have done everything you can, Alex. Nobody could have done anything more."

Nesterov looked up, realizing that Amosov had just said something to him.

"What?"

Felix Amosov looked distraught; his boss slipping off into space like this made him anxious. Signs of weakness at this point could put everyone in danger. He popped another piece of nicotine gum into his mouth, glanced over to Ostankino, who was already coming to the end of his own cigarette, then looked back to his boss and friend.

"*Nichevo!* The fight is over. We have lost. We have to move on with business."

Nesterov shot a barbed look towards Amosov. "*Nichevo?* Do you understand the implications here? We still have three days to find Freeman!"

Amosov shook his head. "Alex, we do not have anything... zero. They are so high on security down at the FBI that our people cannot even water the plants in the same town!"

Nesterov placed his hands down firmly on the desk, leaning forward towards his two men. "The only way we can save Danny at this point is to get Freeman to recant his testimony. I do not give a *govno* how you find him—or what you do to him to get him to change his story. I want everyone we have on this. Do I make myself clear?"

Amosov and Ostankino nodded simultaneously.

"And if he does not surface?" Amosov inquired.

Nesterov glared back at both men.

"Then we are in for a bloodbath."

iii

A light, mystic rain began to fall upon the Kingdom. Chumael, shunning the shelter, stood in the center of the mist. He allowed the droplets to fall upon his face, not quite quenching his deep thirst.

The remaining members of the choir had gathered inside, and Machiel called from the threshold.

"My brother, Choirmaster, the others have assembled."

Chumael glanced absently towards Machiel. "Then let us begin."

The twelve began their multi-layered praise of their Sovereign—the

PHOENIX

One who was now doing something *new*. Though in many ways their collective praise always brought about something fresh among them, this day something was different. For a moment, the praise ceased.

"Sh'ma!"

"What is this?" Gibrael said incredulously.

Chumael looked at Gibrael, clearly unconcerned. "What is *what*, my brother?"

"I sensed it too." It was Orofiel who spoke this time.

"Something has changed," Rephiel injected. "But it is not a...a Sovereign-like new birth change. It is a change, but it is not new. It is resembling a *lessening* of something good."

"Do you *fear* change, my brother?" Chumael spoke in a manner which struck all present as... *different.*

Machiel spoke up. "My brother, Chumael. You speak in a word which we do not know. In this word... in this praise, there is an *absence.*"

"The Sovereign has done something new, my brothers," Chumael responded. "Let us not hesitate to emulate Him." Then after looking across the others, he said, "Let us be in unity, shall we again begin?"

But the absence deepened.

2

I ask you...
>When can two be one?

A dichotomous state
Exists
Only
Through the refusal to acknowledge
>...one's darker twin.

The great abyss
Which separates the two
Has grown
>Smaller
No longer aspiring
To condone the doctrine
Which divides my Temple.

Thrice
Have I fallen
Only to rise again
Destroying the very bridge
Which I had once built
>Once nurtured
>Once feared.

Though banished to darkness
This entity
Would importune its antipode
For but one glimpse
Of eternity

PHOENIX

Yet
Still
Would relish the opportunity
    To reign once again

For
It knows
As now, do I
That the Final Frontier
    Exists within ourselves.

I alone
Abide within the chasm
And
Though I once felt certain of the soil
    on which I stood
I can no longer discern
My Right
    From my Left.

          – J.C.S.
          Integrity

i

Nathan handed his personally rolled joint to Jenny Carlin, who was sitting to his immediate right. They had grown bored with the graduation ceremony the minute they sat down and felt it only fair that they provide entertainment for those not so academically inclined. Namely, themselves.

He pulled a pair of shades from the waistband of his boxers and placed them on, protecting his now bloodshot eyes from the intensity of the sun.

A voice blared out across the public address system.

"...and at this time, it gives me great pleasure to introduce to you our salutatorian of the graduating class. This student had the distinction of being the class president, lettering in three sports, and maintaining the second highest grade point average in the school. Additionally, he has been granted a full scholarship to Kent State University. I give to you Jonathan Storm."

Nathan jerked up in his seat, losing what was left of the roach he was milking. He stood up and let out a loud roar, prompting the remainder of the graduating class to oblige Jonathan with a standing ovation.

Jonathan was momentarily caught off-guard by the reception. Though he enjoyed a positive reputation with the entire student body, it was a bit of a shock to have that friendship affirmed in such a manner.

He approached the podium, clasping the outstretched hand of the assistant principal, the greatly reviled, and somewhat feared, Joran Waddock. Jonathan unfolded his prepared speech and placed it out in front of him, clearing his throat as he did so. Though he had tried to block it from his mind, he still heard Nathan's voice echoing in his head.

"What kind of crap speech is that?"

Nathan had never been one to hold his opinion to himself. After reading his speech to Nathan three days prior, Jonathan had instantly regretted it.

"So that will be it?" Nathan had said. *"You're just going to waltz off with your high-class friends and sell your soul to the rat race?"*

This statement had hurt Jonathan. He himself had been thinking about what it would be like to not be around Nathan—perhaps never again to be together. They were the only brothers each other had.

"So what would you have me do?" Jonathan had responded in anguish.

Nathan's response was one which Jonathan knew he would be unable to shake. With a look of extreme intensity on his face, Nathan had answered the question posed by his best friend without missing a beat.

"Follow my lead."

Jonathan looked up, realizing the silence had extended beyond what would be considered a comfortable dramatic pause. He looked back to Assistant Principal Waddock, who attempted to return an expression of encouragement but was unable to hide his own perplexed thoughts. Jonathan looked down at his speech, then gazed out across the ocean of students and parents. With a deep breath, he picked up the paper from the podium, crumpled it up and tossed it off to the side.

There was some murmuring in the audience, and one student even released a piercing "Ye-haw". It was not difficult for Jonathan to discern Nathan's voice.

Jonathan cleared his throat. "Ah... how's everybody doing today?" he asked weakly.

There was some chuckling in the audience. Jonathan took another deep breath and then smiled—only for an instant—to himself.

"I had a nice, stuffy and boring speech for you today. It was something about how 'we are the future of the world.' I suppose I'd imagined myself giving a moving speech on God and Country, leaving you all with proud tears in your eyes. I know I had my mom crying after reading it for the two hundredth time in front of the mirror."

A lighthearted laughter broke out, and Jonathan was finally able to spot Nathan looking up at him, sporting a grin of approval. He continued.

"Well, a goodhearted friend of mine let me know, in a manner which I don't think I can share in mixed company, that my speech was full of hot air. I appreciate that, Nate, you're like the older brother I never wanted."

Another burst of laughter erupted from the audience.

Jonathan smiled and then shifted on his feet, feeling a bit lightheaded. As he stared out across the crowd, the words began to come to him as clear as day. A serious look came across his face.

"Things are changing..."

The audience ceased to murmur, sensing the transformation in his tone.

"The world is moving on. In order that we appreciate just how, it's necessary that we allow ourselves to see the signs of the times. The Islamic Revolution of Europe... our own 'New Independence Act', which has left the United States 'secure', yet isolated from the rest of the world... the 'Great Recession' and subsequent 'Second Depression', which has allowed much of our nation to more resemble the third world than the superpower it once was... yes, things are changing. The world *is* moving on... and really, what are *we* going to do about it?"

He felt something begin to well up inside of him, a sense of discord, which he quickly pushed back down before continuing.

"As a class, we have now ended our instructional years. The time for foolishness and carefree days is now gone, never to be recovered. So too have we as a people of this world completed our childhood. The time is at hand... the rent is now due."

Jonathan gazed out across the multitude of people. Every eye was fixed upon him. Yet, the only face he seemed to notice was that of Nathan's. An expression of calm encouragement remained fixed on his countenance. Even more so, it was an expression of understanding.

"Decisions have been made for us up until this time. A multitude of choices lie ahead. However seemingly ambiguous they may appear, each choice moves us either closer to, or further from, our ultimate goal. Before today, we could not help but be the products of these past decisions of others. Yet, on this day I say to you all, our choices from this moment forward will shape our futures, both in this world and the next. We live in the latter days, and where we choose to make our stand, be it in darkness or in light, the day is ours to embrace."

Jonathan felt a surge of energy within him as he spoke his final phrase. "Thank you all, and God bless."

Amidst a deafening silence, Jonathan walked from the podium and stepped down from the stage. He moved through the center aisle, yet he did not stop at the end of the student section. He continued to walk straight through the crowd, seemingly in a daze. No one said a word; everyone instead sat mesmerized. No one that is except for Nathan, who had silently slipped away from the crowd and was now walking off towards the woods, providing encouragement and solace, to the one person in the world he could truly call "friend."

ii

Danny Caputo sat stone-faced as synthetic leather straps were fastened around his wrists and ankles. He had just spoken to Father Ebright and given his Act of Contrition. Despite living nearly seven decades in one form of peril or another, Caputo was terrified, yet he was determined not to allow anyone present to verify this fact.

He watched as the witnesses filed into a room behind a plate-glass viewing window. The prison guard placed the electrode helmet over his head. Years of technology had led the country to more "compassionate" means of terminating the lives of these wretched souls, but in an attempt to curb the surge in violence following the national economic, as well as social, collapse, less "civilized" means had been brought back. All states now had capital punishment instituted as part of their "suite" of criminal sanctions. Most had these events televised or open to the general public. A few states had brought back the firing squad. One had even reintroduced hanging.

Caputo felt cheated, no doubt. In a society that was now ripe for high levels of organized crime, he had been singled out as an example for the rest, proof that the government was turning the tide.

It just isn't fair, he thought.

As the remainder of the prison staff went about their business, preparing for this "glorious" event scheduled to take place in less than five minutes, the prison guard whispered something into Caputo's ear.

"What did you say?" Caputo responded in a voice somewhat louder than a whisper.

"I said," the guard continued from just outside of the range of Caputo's peripheral vision. "Do not change the expression on your face, and for the love of the devil, do *not* act as if you're talking to me. I have important information for you."

Caputo allowed his eyes to wander across the room. Strangely enough, no one else seemed to be paying attention to him and this mysterious prison guard. With his eyes fixed on the warden to his left, Caputo whispered back.

"Go on."

The guard continued to check all the connections to the chair in which Caputo sat. "Nesterov located the Freeman family three weeks ago but gave the order for his men not to take any action."

Caputo fought against an instinctive look of astonishment. "What the hell do you mean he found Freeman? Alexandre would have informed me if this were true. Who the hell are you anyway?"

The guard slid around to the front of the chair, looking Caputo straight in the eyes while feigning an adjustment to the electrodes on his head. Caputo could have sworn that the guard that he had come in with was no more than thirty-five or thirty-six years old, with jet-black hair, but this man before him was perhaps in his late forties—if not older—with strands of gray.

"I guess you could say that I was once a friend of the Nesterov family," he breathed. "I can get you out of this, Danny, but I need something from you first."

"I don't believe it," Caputo muttered, maintaining the poker face that had made him famous. "Alexandre would never betray me like that. I've known him for thirty…"

"Forget what you might have thought, old man." The supposed guard looked into Caputo's eyes with an expression of intense hatred. "Alexandre Nesterov is at this very moment putting together his boys to assure his succession to you. He's become very comfortable in his position these past few years while you sat rotting away in prison."

Caputo could no longer hide the look of disdain on his face. "I just can't believe that Alex would—"

"Give it up, Danny-boy. You know what they say about absolute power. Anyway, as you can see, I'm here and his boys are not." The man gave his statement time to sink in. "So who you gonna go with, my friend?"

Caputo hesitated. He bit his lower lip as he continued to scan the room. Why the hell was no one paying attention to him? Wasn't he tonight's main attraction?

Caputo released a heavy, yet frustrated, sigh. "What do you want from me?"

The guard smiled—a smile that gave Caputo shivers.

"Just one… *meager* piece of information."

"Name it!" Caputo whispered anxiously, clenching his teeth.

"The location of Nesterov's daughter, Vanya."

Caputo began to turn his head towards the man but quickly ceased the motion. "What do you want with Vanya?"

"That," the man replied, "is not your concern, Danny-boy. Two thousand volts, and a dozen or so amps, is!"

Caputo thought quickly to himself. Could it be possible that Nesterov had turned on him? It wouldn't be the first time one of his men had. But Alex? That was hard to believe. Then again… how long had it been since he had received any communication from good old Alexandre? Three weeks? Maybe four? And when was the last time he, or anyone else in the Nesterov family for that matter, had come to visit him?

Caputo felt a rush of thoughts and scenarios entering his head which had never occurred to him before. Though they had worked together for nearly thirty years, did the ambitious really have any friends?

PHOENIX

Caputo inquired nervously, "You can get me out of here?"

The guard grinned. "In the wink of an eye."

"Okay... I don't know exactly where she is, but it's in North Carolina. I know this because Alex flies into Raleigh-Durham Airport when he goes to visit her. Nesterov's grandson is there with her... must be about eighteen by now. Kid's had some serious problems... some ritualistic child abuse, anyway now he—"

Caputo stopped short, now realizing he was center stage again. The warden looked at him, then over to the staff member sitting at the switch. Caputo threw his gaze back to the guard at his side, but...

This was not the older man whom he had just spoken to; instead it was the younger guard he had entered the room with. Caputo looked desperately to the right and then shot back to his left. His gaze returned to the warden, who slowly turned his head away and nodded.

Caputo had just enough time to urinate on himself before the clock hit 12:01 a.m.

3

Allied Press ~

JERUSALEM, Israel — In an unprecedented event, Prime Minister Menachem Ashir of Israel has appointed a Christian to a major cabinet post. Eliot Kohein Lige will assume his duties as Foreign Minister of Israel sometime next week.

Lige is best known for his leadership in the grass roots movement, *Christians of Israel*, a contemporary Messianic Jewish movement. This movement has been credited with the rapid expansion of Christians returning to the Holy Land. It is estimated that nearly two million European citizens have immigrated to Israel under the terms of the Eurabic-Old Europe Non-Aggression Accord, following the Islamic Revolution in Europe. The military expulsion of all Muslims from Israel created an economic and workforce vacuum that was easily filled through this immigration.

Lige, though Christian, is ethnically Jewish, and states he converted after "coming to know Christ". In the past seven years, Israel's Christian people have grown to twenty seven percent of the population.

PHOENIX

i

Jonathan pulled onto Trinity Street, as he had done ten thousand times before. However, though he usually pulled into the third driveway on the right, nearly three-dozen cars prevented him from doing so on this occasion. Nathan had been determined to throw "the Mother of all Bashes" this graduation night, and it appeared that all was going according to plan. The perimeter of the property was lined with additional security guards, all carrying automatic rifles, each probably more likely to shoot himself in the foot if any truly dangerous situation arose, yet still filling the role of "deterrent".

Jonathan waved to some friends as he found an open spot a block down. Even from his parking space, he could hear Nathan's band plugging away its own version of classic punk-thrash rock. Besides being the final farewell to high school, Nathan had announced the planned demise of his group *Sex Sex Sex and the Love Pumps* after the party.

Jonathan entered through the front gate after confirming his identity with the guards and then went straight through to the front door, greeting several fellow graduates as he made his way to the back door.

Matt Kohl called out to him from across the room. "Hey, Jon-boy! Heads up!"

A can of Curés-light beer sailed across the room, which Jonathan snagged out of the air with his right hand.

"Touchdown!" Matt yelled jubilantly as he moved towards Jonathan. "I tell you, Storm, whether on the gridiron or at the bash of the year, we're still a heck of a connection!"

Jonathan smiled and shook Matt's hand. "And I suppose twenty years from now you'll still be talking about that ball you under-threw in the Claymont game."

"Under-threw?" Matt feigned being hurt. "You dropped it! I hit you right in the numbers!"

"Matt, you broke my foot."

Matt unfurled a slight grimace. "Aww... who can remember ancient history anyway? Say, Jon, that was some speech today. What the hell did it mean?"

Jonathan provided a good-natured smile. "You know, Matt, I kind of wonder that myself."

He glanced outside as he popped open the beer his friend had tossed him. "How long has the band been playing?" he asked.

Matt looked at his watch. "They started at about ten... it's been almost three hours." Then looking at Jonathan, he winked. "I think this is his final set though; our prayers have been answered."

"Well," Jonathan began, turning towards the back door, "I don't want to miss what's left of the final farewell tour. Take it easy, Matt."

"The only way I can!"

Jonathan walked out the back sliding door, hearing Nathan rip away on his guitar. Nathan spotted him entering the backyard and winked as he cut into the final verse of his closing song.

> *"Screw all the virgins and their mothers too*
> *Take whatever they won't give to you*
> *Run from no one, send their hearts to Hell*
> *Bludgeon your parents and you'll feel quite well!*
>
> *I'll put a pitchfork in your heart!"*

The band finished with a deafening crescendo, then cut off. Amidst the cheers from the near two hundred students in attendance, Nathan hopped off the stage and scooted through the crowd towards Jonathan.

"Jonny-boy!" He called out as he reached his friend. "So what did you think?"

Jonathan shook his head, not completely amused. "Where do you come up with all that satanic stuff, Nate?"

Nathan smiled. "Something I picked up in my younger years, big guy. Besides, we are, I mean *were*, strictly a satirical band. You *do* know what satire is Jon-boy, don't you?"

"All I can say, Nate, is that if there is a devil, I'm sure he's listening."

"Oh there *is*, Jonny," Nathan muttered, "there is."

Jonathan had always found it curious how Nathan, a sworn atheist, still seemed to hold a paradoxical belief in evil. Their brief conversation was interrupted by Paula Sauerbrey, Nathan's former girlfriend.

"Hey boys! Great finale, Nathan... or should I say *Sex Sex Sex*?" She looked towards Jonathan. "Trust me, Jon, no girl that ever dated him would have dubbed him that, and there have been a few."

Jonathan displayed a polite grin while Nathan did his best to fabricate a wounded expression. The three then spontaneously broke into laughter.

When their mirth concluded, Nathan turned to Jonathan. "Listen, Jon, I've got to mingle a bit. I just want to make sure we're still on for the soup kitchen tomorrow."

"Yes... tomorrow... next week, and every week until the end of time, oh great one," Jonathan remarked. "So I'm praying for Armageddon, Nate, that you might have your license reinstated."

"And then I'll be a regular hell-on-wheels once again! Now, if you'll excuse me."

Nathan saluted, clicking his heels, and then moved off through the crowd.

Paula's gaze remained with Nathan for a few moments, then she looked back towards Jonathan with a thoughtful expression. "You know, Jon, from the way he looks, I'd say Nathan is the last person I'd expect to be volunteering in a soup kitchen. You know what I mean?"

Jonathan nodded pensively. "It's just his overdone exterior, Paula. You know better than anyone that's not the full Nate."

"Yes, I do know..." Paula paused nostalgically. "Nathan was probably the most caring guy I ever went with. Bizarre, yet caring. But still, spending sometimes five days a week down there? I mean, that's way more than his probation requires. What gives?"

Jonathan shrugged. "Well, Nate told me that some people really helped him out when his family was in need some years ago. I guess he's just trying to give something back."

With the band having completed its set, the latest dance music began to play out from the audio system.

Paula shook her head. "I guess it's just too much for me to figure out tonight." She turned towards Jonathan with an anticipatory smile. "Dance with me, Jon?"

"It would be my honor."

ii

Vanya was in the woods again. She had been having this same dream, more nights than she could count, since that horrible night when she lost Tobias. She would be lying, paralyzed amongst a thick brush, as the serpent slithered through the trees.

"Vaaaaanyaaaaa," it hissed.

This was no ordinary serpent, however. Vanya recognized his face from day one as that of Luther. He would move methodically through the trees, searching for her and Jesse. From her hiding place, Vanya could see the serpent's bloated belly. She watched, tearfully, as the bulge wriggled and writhed, pressing itself up against the inside of the serpent's skin. Once pressed against the scaly sheath, Vanya could discern the features of a small boy.

At this point in the dream, each time Vanya would have to bite down on her tongue to prevent herself from crying out. It would become too emotionally excruciating, though, as the serpent opened its jaws and instead of the expected sound of a reptile's hiss, Vanya would hear the cries of a small child.

"Nanny Vanya! Please come and get me... I'm scared... he's hurting me. It hurts so bad, Nanny Vanya, please help me, pl—"

Then the serpent's jaws would crash shut, and he would proceed with his search.

But something was different this time. At this point in the dream, when Vanya felt as if she was at her weakest, the serpent would usually continue to slither by, coming within a breath of her hiding place, but still never finding her. This time, however, a wicked smile broke out across the jaws of the serpent, sending a freezing chill down Vanya's spine.

"Vaaanyaaaa," it hissed. *"I can smell you. It won't be long now!"*

The serpent turned, and in the blink of an eye, spun on its belly, sweeping down and bringing itself face-to-face with Vanya, its fiendish jaws only centimeters away.

"You are MINE!"

iii

Father Daniel was no more than a block from his parish when the police officer stopped him on the sidewalk.

"Father, what do you think you're doing?"

"I'm returning from a visit to a parishioner. She's sick, and I don't need to tell you that medicine is scarce. I was giving her the comfort of the Sacraments."

The police officer frowned. "That isn't what I meant, Father. You're out in public with your Roman collar exposed. You know the law regarding the public display of any religion."

"I'm a priest."

"Yes, and I'm an officer of the law. You know the *law*, I'm sure, Father."

"Yes. I know the law of the land, but even more so, I know the law of God. He says if you are ashamed of Me before others, then I too will be ashamed before you on that Day of Judgment. Do you understand that you too will be subject to this judgment, Officer…"

"Orieton. And Father, you can practice your religion with total freedom in your church and on private property, so long as you aren't in view of others. I realize that makes your job a bit more—"

"Not my job, my vocation."

"Whatever you want to call it, Father. But after those religionists set off that dirty bomb in our own city—and what with the nationwide torching of Mosques by many people of *your own group*, you, of all people, should understand the need for discretion."

"I understand only the need for love. I understand only the need for Christ."

"That's your opinion and your religion, Father." The officer's indignation grew. "Forcing it on others and presenting it as the *only* way is what has caused the bulk of the problems in the world. Your 'Christ' has been the source of more war and misery in the world than just about any other person in the history of humanity."

"With all due respect, Officer Orieton, *we* cannot lay blame on Christ for what we have done."

The officer shook his head in disgust. "With all due respect, *Father*, you put your faith in a dead man."

"I put my faith in love, and He that *is* love." With that, Father Daniel pulled out a crucifix and held it before the officer. "And perhaps you may ask yourself, why we have chosen to nail love to a cross!"

4

When once the Soule has lost her way,
O then, how restless does she stray!
And having not her Guide for light,
How does she erre in endlesse night!

– Robert Herrick

i

Luther stood at the altar, surrounded in a semicircle by the *Illumini*. Glowing candles filled the room as a hundred or so close associates approached the altar with gifts. It was his fiftieth birthday, but perhaps even more importantly, it was the fifth anniversary of the Day of Communion.

Luther chanted a few passages, then sat down in his seat behind the altar. The twenty additional members of the *Illumini* knelt at his side as the offerings were placed on and around the altar.

He inhaled deeply, enjoying the aroma and hypnotic sensation flowing from the incense. Once the last offering had been placed, he rose again, addressing his congregation.

"Children of the Great Seraph," he began. "I thank you for your participation in this most joyous event. Today we celebrate the Day of Communion, where the Brotherhood, once divided, now stands united as one under our Master. No longer are we a series of petty sideshows, clouded in ignorance and pseudo-rituals. We are strong, as we must be to prepare for what is to come.

"For the day is near where one greater than I approaches. He shall live and breathe as do you and I, but He will be like no other man. He shall be *The Opposer Incarnate*, and as sure as I stand before you, dominion of the Earth will be His!"

A wind swept through the Temple, extinguishing the multitude of candles. The congregation looked forward, witnessing the low-level glow emanating from Luther. The *Illumini*, also luminescent, stood and moved forward.

"I am but a voice crying out from the fire. Guide us, Master, as we seek out your Anointed," Luther chanted. "For it is your will which must be followed, not ours."

A brilliant flash temporarily blinded all in attendance. A moment later, they opened their eyes to see all the candles once again lit. However, Luther and the *Illumini* no longer stood before them.

They had vanished.

ii

"We have to go, Alex!" Felix Amosov urged.

Nesterov continued to sit in his chair and stare off into space. He was having a difficult time swallowing the news he had just been given.

His voice squeaked in a whisper. "Any idea who is claiming responsibility?"

Amosov looked down. "I am pretty sure it was from within."

Nesterov turned his head, wincing at the words spoken by his confidant. He was determined not to cry; yet he would have to do something about this overwhelming pain.

"He never really wanted a part of my world," he murmured absently. "He did not step into it until the situation with Vanya and Marisha. In fact, I know he secretly hated me for who I was... still... he was my son."

Nesterov covered his face with both hands. Amosov stood a moment, feeling awkward being in Nesterov's presence at such an emotionally difficult juncture. He slid slowly into the seat in front of the desk.

"Have you told Annie yet?"

Nesterov clenched his eyes tightly, imagining the task which stood before him. *She* was the one who truly hated him for what he was. Yet she stood by him, as her intense religious beliefs prevented her from seeking a divorce. How was he to tell this mother that the second of her three children was dead, and that he was to blame?

"Yerik…"

"Alex, it is not safe for you here anymore." Amosov interrupted his thoughts. "We must get you out of here."

Nesterov leaned back in his chair and crossed his arms. He shook his head, his eyes now glistening with tears, and stared off into space again.

"What is the point…?" he mumbled.

"Alexandre?" Amosov questioned, an expression of concern on his face.

Nesterov stared for another few moments, then, taking a deep breath, he turned towards Amosov. Their eyes locked momentarily, and Amosov could see his friend's executive side begin to re-emerge.

"How many do we have loyal to me?"

"With all things being considered," Amosov began, "Of course Gavrilenkov, but after him, I would say we have a dozen more which I would trust."

Nesterov initially looked shocked, then despondent. "That is it?"

"Listen, Alex, we are at a point where I do not put anything past anybody. Loyalties are divided… stories are being circulated. We cannot risk a large circle of confidants."

Nesterov nodded solemnly. He knew Amosov was right. His failure to save Caputo had been viewed as a sign of weakness by many, but he was unsure if that was worse than the rumors that he had actually *wanted* Caputo out of the way so that he might take over the syndicate.

"All right, get Ostankino on the line and let's get moving," he instructed.

Amosov hesitated. Nesterov looked up to see a look of derision on Felix's face. "What is it?"

"It's Mikhail. He was held in high favor with Caputo. He hasn't checked in in the past five days. I think he is…"

Nesterov interrupted angrily. "Are you suggesting what I think you are, Felix? Because I am not sure I want to hear it! Mikhail Ostankino has been loyal to me for almost ten years, he is——"

"He has been an opportunistic *sooka* since the day you brought him on. That ass-kissing smokestack is no son of Russia, he must spend an hour every morning trying to make himself look more American. I am telling you, Alex, power is shifting, and he desires to shift with it. He is not to be trusted at this point."

Nesterov felt like a thousand-kilo weight had been dropped on his chest. Could it be possible that Ostankino would betray him? Or was it more likely that Amosov was looking out for his own interests? He eyed Amosov suspiciously, questioning his motives in his own mind.

Amosov and Ostankino never had seemed particularly fond of each other, both displaying a certain air of competition between them. And it had been Amosov, more so than Ostankino, who had questioned Nesterov's orders, albeit in private. It could be possible. Amosov could be...

Nesterov jerked himself, ending this line of thought.

Chyort voz'mi! What is happening to me? What am I thinking?

iii

Nathan was lost again.

He sprinted down the street, hearing the voices from the mob of people chasing him, perhaps only a few dozen meters behind. They were gaining.

Nathan ran up to the front door of a house, pounding on it.

"Help me!" he screamed.

He looked towards the window and saw the face of a woman. He jumped back in horror as he realized her eyes were completely white. A dreamy, yet terrifying voice slithered from her parched lips.

"You've been discovered. It's over. For all of us."

His head jerked as a car horn blared from behind him.

"Ahhh!" he screamed.

PHOENIX

Nathan realized he was sitting up in his bed covered in a cold sweat. He closed his eyes and took a deep breath. A car horn honked again, and he jumped.

"Nate! Train's a-rollin'!"

It was Jonathan's voice. Nathan hopped out of bed and popped his head out the window. Jonathan was sitting in his convertible with a mild expression of concern on his face. Masias, the security guard, looked up awkwardly at the scene.

"Sorry, Jon. I overslept... I'll be down in five."

He did not give Jonathan an opportunity to respond before sprinting to the shower.

It was actually seven minutes before Nathan made it to the car.

"You're going to be late to your own funeral," Jonathan stated sarcastically.

"That may be sooner than you think, ol' boy," Nathan responded absently, climbing into the car.

Jonathan pulled out into the street, nodding to Masias as he closed the gate, and then began the five-kilometer drive to the soup kitchen. He looked over at Nathan, who seemed preoccupied with something.

"Something wrong, Nate?"

Nathan looked slowly towards his friend and shrugged his shoulders. "Nothing I can't handle, buddy."

Jonathan was used to this behavior. While Nathan was a happy-go-lucky friend ninety percent of the time, he did have his moments where he seemed to completely cut everyone else off. Over the years Jonathan had learned that, whatever inner-demons Nathan was battling at these times, they were not something he cared to talk about.

"So," Jonathan began, "how long before the judge gives you your license back?" He knew the answer to this question, but wanted to get some conversation going to get Nathan's mind off whatever was bothering him.

Nathan produced a mild chuckle and looked at Jonathan for the first time since he had entered the car. "You getting tired of giving me rides, Jon-boy?"

"No, that's not it at all..." Jonathan blurted out. "It's just that—"

"I know, I know. I'm just yanking your chain." Nathan smiled. "Less than a month. Then I've got to take monthly potty tests for a year to keep it. I'm going to have to find a new drug."

Jonathan shook his head. "You know, Nate, sometimes I think you have a death wish. Some of the things you do are just plain insane. Like that time you—"

"Is this going to become another lecture, *Dad?*"

Jonathan looked away, shaking his head once again. He should have known better. When Nathan got into these moods, he became quite hypersensitive.

Nathan continued on, mistaking Jonathan's expression as condescending. "What are you thinking, Jon-boy? 'How is poor old Nate going to survive while I'm off in college?'"

Jonathan glared at him. "No, I'm not." He seemed offended. "To be honest with you, I've been thinking about not even—"

"JON, LOOK OUT!" Nathan screamed.

Jonathan looked back to the road to see a truck heading straight towards them in their lane. He swerved his car up onto the sidewalk in an attempt to avoid a head-on collision. The truck clipped the back end of the driver's side of the car, throwing Jonathan against his window and Nathan into the dashboard.

The truck kept moving for another thirty meters before Jonathan heard a loud crash, followed by a disconcerting thud. He realized they had come to a full stop less than a meter in front of an elm tree. Jonathan was in a bit of a daze as he began to rub his forehead. He looked over to see Nathan with a gash on his head; a light, yet steady flow of blood streamed from it.

"Asshole!" Nathan stated in disbelief, staring at the blood on his hands.

Why didn't the air-bag system deploy?

Jonathan quickly became aware of people shouting from behind them. He turned around to see a horde of people gathering forty meters back. Though he had managed to avoid the brunt of the collision, the car behind him had not been so lucky. Apparently the driver had tried to veer into the opposing traffic lane to avoid the truck, at the same time that the truck driver was able to navigate back to his own lane.

The truck driver stumbled out of the cab then fell to his knees. He was obviously intoxicated. The young woman in the nearly crushed convertible got out, miraculously unhurt due to the air bag, yet still bearing a complexion that was as white as snow. A second woman, slightly older, also emerged from the passenger seat of vehicle. It was then that Jonathan realized that someone had been sitting in the back, unrestrained.

"Oh my God..." Nathan stated in a distressed tone.

Still feeling a bit disoriented, Jonathan turned slightly to see what Nathan had spotted. There, about twenty meters from the car, lay a little girl. Though Jonathan was still a good distance from the child he could see that her face and body were disfigured. A pool of blood was beginning to develop underneath the girl's head as a crowd of bystanders assembled around her.

"My baby!" the young woman screamed as she tried to run towards the child. A man in the crowd mercifully stopped her, trying to shield her from the inevitable truth—that her little girl was already gone.

Jonathan felt a strange tingling sensation emanating from within him. But instead of feeling like he was going to black out, he felt as if his entire body now weighed only a few grams. He slid out of the car, watching as the scene transitioned into slow motion. He moved towards the crowd languorously, feeling as if the entire world existed somewhere off in the distance.

Some phrases from the crowd slipped through his auditory senses, infiltrating the outer reaches of his consciousness.

"She's not breathing..."

"Her head's been crushed..."

"She's gone..."

As he moved closer to the crowd, a middle-aged gentleman turned towards him, looked at him in a funny sort of way, and then moved aside. Another person, and then another, followed suit. By the time Jonathan reached the edge of the crowd, a pathway had been cleared from him to the girl. Everyone was silent, and he felt as if he were looking at the entire scene through a long, dark tunnel.

Jonathan reached the mangled girl and knelt beside her, not knowing exactly what to do. He was, however, certain of one thing, this girl was not going to die.

He felt energy coursing through his veins, from his chest, through his shoulder, and out through the hand which now lay on the girl's forehead.

As he knelt, Jonathan became aware of the pool of blood receding. The bone fragments beneath his hand began to move. The little girl's chest expanded as she breathed inward. Her eyes fluttered momentarily and then opened. All traces of her injuries had miraculously vanished.

The girl sat up as Jonathan stood and took a step backwards.

The young mother finally burst through the crowd and wrapped herself around her daughter, crying uncontrollably.

"I'm hungry," the girl mumbled to her mother.

"Oh, Providence… Oh, my Providence…"

Jonathan continued to step backwards, at an utter loss as to what had just happened. The crowd stared at him in amazement as he slowly became more aware of his surroundings. A man holding a rosary knelt on one knee before him. He gazed upwards, yearningly, at Jonathan's face. Several more followed the man's lead, and in a few moments, the entire crowd was kneeling at Jonathan's feet.

It was at this time that Jonathan became aware of Nathan's hand gripping his arm.

"Let's get the hell out of here!" Nathan whispered insistently as he pulled his friend towards the car.

Jonathan's eyes remained fixated upon the crowd.

Standing about fifty meters away beside his car, Samuel Hagarot put down his camera and scribbled a few notes to himself. He got back into his car, performed a three-point turn in the middle of the street and sped off.

5

And here was a shock the Rooster did not notice:
the wood was naked.

All in a fortnight the trees had lost their leaves to
the ripping wind.

Autumn is the killing season.

– Walter Wangerin, Jr.
The Book of Sorrows

i

The short, stout man sat across the desk from Luther, glancing out the window as Luther silently toiled. Though it was still midsummer, he would be damned if it did not look like a brisk day in the early fall.

Luther sat behind his desk, pouring over a dozen or so pictures that had been presented to him. He stared at each one meticulously, occasionally nodding to himself. As he sorted through the photographs, he was unable to stop a menacing grin from forming on his face.

Without looking up, Luther spoke. "And how long ago did you say these pictures were taken?"

The man abruptly ended his brief reverie and responded. "Two days ago. One of our own was driving just outside a town called Pergamum when he witnessed this... 'incident'. Kid's name is Hagarot, Samuel Hagarot. A real prodigy... maybe the most creative person I've ever met. He does photography as a hobby, but it's really music that's his—"

The man stopped instantly as he noted Luther's raised hand, coupled with an intense glare that seemed like he was looking right through him.

"Senator…"

William Maison had never in his many meetings with Luther seen the man so vexed, even at a loss for words.

"This boy… Hagarot… he would be what, about seventeen or eighteen?"

Maison nodded. "Yeah, I think he's seventeen. Finished high school two years ago. He actually sought us out. Ambitious, multitalented, but a bit moody for my taste. Still, somehow he was just at the right place at the right—"

"Enough!"

Maison again halted his speaking, as the clearly disturbed Luther stood from his desk and began to wander about the room.

The whore never told me! And then… still giving him the name 'Samuel'.

He turned to Maison, regathering his thoughts, attempting to focus on the primary concern of his son, Jesse.

"I will be interested to learn more of the boy Samuel at another time. For now, I require that his activities and whereabouts be monitored. I may have other… assignments for him." Luther breathed deeply as he returned to his seat behind the desk. "What I want to know now is the name this boy in the pictures uses."

"Well, my lord, we took down the license plate number and traced the car's ownership to an oil company out of Texas. I'll be damned if we could get any more information than that."

Luther cocked an eyebrow as he looked up at Maison. "Indeed?" He paused as he looked away towards the blank wall. "Tell me, Senator, what is the closest major airport to this town of… what did you call it… Pergamum?"

Maison thought for a moment. "Hard to say, probably Wilmington, North Carolina."

Luther paused before speaking again. "And if you did not want it to be known that you were heading to Pergamum, what would be a less obvious airport into which to fly?"

The man paused only for an instant. "It'd have to be either Norfolk, Virginia or Raleigh-Durham."

Luther smiled. "Very well. I want you to head back to Washington immediately. You have served us well."

PHOENIX

The senator nodded respectfully and exited the room. Three men entered a moment later, whom Luther immediately addressed. "I am going to narrow the focus of our search to a fifty kilometer radius around Pergamum, North Carolina. And I want you to retrieve this photographer; I need to speak with him, soon."

ii

"I don't know what's going on, Dr. I.," Jonathan stated in a despondent tone.

He sat in a chair directly across from Dr. Viktor Ilyushenko, yet he seemed to be more interested in looking at his own shoes.

Dr. Ilyushenko looked steadily at him. "Have you been dreaming about your brother again, Jonathan?"

Tears came to Jonathan's eyes as he slowly nodded.

"How many times this month?" the doctor inquired.

Jonathan sniffled. "I don't know... ten.... maybe twelve times."

Ilyushenko sat back and raised an eyebrow. "They have become much more frequent. I had thought they were just about over."

Jonathan nodded, a tear finally breaking free and sliding down his cheek.

Ilyushenko leaned forward again. "Tell me, Jonathan, has anything changed? What is it that Tobias is saying to you in the dreams?"

Jonathan brought his hand up to wipe his eyes as additional tears began streaming down. "He's got that knife st-stuck in his ch-chest, and he looks at me and says that it sh-should have been me."

Ilyushenko nodded. "You still bear a great deal of guilt over your brother's death, do you not?"

Jonathan looked up with a taste of agitation. "Doc, how can't I?" Quickly becoming more impassioned, Jonathan stood up and walked to the back corner of the room, where Dr. Ilyushenko's endless collection of psychiatry books rested on the many shelves.

"I graduated last month. I got a scholarship. I gave a speech. I should have been real proud of myself. But instead, all I could think about was 'this should have been Toby.' The feeling has grown, Dr. I. It's gotten worse. And strange things have been happening to me."

Ilyushenko tilted his head inquisitively. "Strange things?"

Jonathan turned back towards the doctor. "Yes, I can't explain it, but a couple of weeks ago there was a car accident."

"Yes," Ilyushenko nodded. "I remember your Aunt Vannie telling me about it."

"Well," Jonathan continued. "What I didn't tell my aunt, or anyone for that matter, was that I went up to a little girl who had been hurt, and I..."

Jonathan stopped himself. Ilyushenko looked at him intently. "You what, Jonathan?"

Jonathan cleared his throat, trying to pull himself out of whatever daze he had been in. He looked directly at the doctor and stated, almost disbelievingly, "I *healed* her."

Ilyushenko was unable to prevent his eyes from showing a brief moment of skepticism. He attempted to disguise this quickly with an expression of concern but was sure he was too late.

"I know, Dr. I.," Jonathan sounded exasperated. "It sounds crazy, but it happened. People saw it, I..."

Jonathan stopped himself again, struggling over the thought that he had made a grave mistake by sharing this with his psychiatrist. It *was* unbelievable. Then again, he had seen many unbelievable things in his short life. He decided, however, that now was not the time to go into all of this.

"I don't know, Dr. I," he said, looking for an out. "Maybe I just bumped my head and imagined the whole thing." He looked up at the clock. "Lord! I promised Aunt Vannie... ahh... my mom that I'd take her shopping today. I've got to run!"

"Jonathan, I think..." Ilyushenko started in, but he was too late. Jonathan was already out the door. He was not sure what to think of all this, but it was quite unsettling.

He took a moment to go to the second-story window, watching as Jonathan Storm, a.k.a. Jesse Chardin, slipped into his car and took off. Perhaps not his most productive session. He would need to do better if he wanted his benefactor to stay happy.

PHOENIX

Viktor Ilyushenko had had his psychiatry practice relocated to the southeast at the request of his long-time friend, Alexandre Nesterov. The truth was, Jonathan was Ilyushenko's only real client. The rest were contacts and phonies as a part of a money-laundering practice for Nesterov, working with a number of powerful drug cartels in the now communist South and Central America.

After witnessing the brutal murder of Tobias, Nesterov had wanted the best for his surviving grandson. He did not want Ilyushenko "wasting emotional energy" on any other clients, so he paid the good doctor a comfortable salary for his one patron. Ilyushenko, up until now, had been happy with the progress Jonathan had made over the past eleven years. But today he was concerned.

He buzzed his secretary on the intercom.

"Del, will you call Vannie Storm and see if you can fit her into my schedule for next week? It is important that I speak with her."

A sarcastic voice rang back across the receiver. "Gee, Dr. I., how am I ever going to fit her into your busy schedule? You might need to come in on Sat—"

Ilyushenko switched off the intercom. He had often regretted hiring his smart-ass daughter-in-law for that position. If she were even the slightest bit pleasant to look at, he might have more tolerance. What his son saw in her he never knew. Probably just a fascination with older American women, surely aided by his penchant for Vodka. Still, Del knew how to keep her mouth shut, and Ilyushenko was a firm believer in the concept of nepotism.

iii

Pope Peter II walked along the beaches of Patmos, rosary in hand, gazing longingly in the direction of the once Christian Europe. It was only by an act of God that he had been able to escape the multiple attempts on his life during the initial stages of the Islamic Revolution; an act of God aided by the ultimate sacrifice of over three hundred Swiss Guards and a gratefully welcomed invitation from the Orthodox Ecumenical Patriarch, Andreas II. In an odd twist of events that even Peter found quite ironic, it was ultimately the Sicilian Mafia that had chartered the boat which carried him to safety on the now sovereign Greek island. Many there had given their lives as well.

DOMINION

A strange sense of loyalty, Peter mused. *And a contradiction in vocation.*

He prayed continually for those who had given their lives for such a wretched soul as he. He offered prayers of gratitude for his host and now co-exile Andreas II. And he lifted up prayers of wonder over the strange Divine protection that enveloped this tiny island, which no hostile force seemed to be able to penetrate by air or sea. It had become a regular Bermuda Triangle for those who wished the Prelate harm.

Msgr. Craig Ebright, the Pontiff's personal assistant and confidant, walked by his side.

"I had a dream last night, Monsignor."

"Yes, Holy Father?"

"Yes, it was of a very holy man. A priest. He was clearly of Middle Eastern descent... perhaps even Persian, yet he spoke in clear English— *American* English."

"The Church suffers a different kind of martyrdom in America, Holy Father."

"Yes, it does, my good Monsignor. And it was suffering that he was, he *is*, called to do. I saw seven people standing behind him... men and women, differing ages. A dragon blew hot fire in their direction. This priest stood between them and was able to deflect most of the fire, yet not all."

"Is that not the calling of all of us, priests and the religious, to protect the flock from the evil one?"

"True, Monsignor, but I sensed that this man had a singular and specific calling. There was one other curious piece of the vision."

"Yes, Holy Father?"

"There was an angel, though he resembled a man, who lay between the dragon and the priest. He was bound from head to foot. He was consistently singed by the flames... his wounds then healing... then singed again."

Msgr. Ebright winced as he reflected on the vision. "Do you know what it all means, Holy Father?"

Peter stopped, then turned around, looking at the footprints in the sand that were now being eroded by the waves. His eyes moved into the dreamy look that the good monsignor had grown accustomed to.

"Monsignor, I am in a place that I never intended to be, in an office I sought, but for all the wrong reasons. Christ, with not a little help from His

Blessed Mother, has for reasons beyond my intellect called me out of the pit and into a different kind of fire. Though the world continues to darken, I sensed a great light in the people from this vision. Some do not know the light they possess as of yet. What can I do but pray?"

"What can any of us do, short of God's grace, Holy Father?"

Peter smiled and nodded. Their walk continued. Peter, moving from less prophetic to more tangible matters, inquired, "Whom do we have the pleasure of meeting today?"

Having the Pontiff's schedule committed to memory, Msgr. Ebright responded, "You have a simple breakfast with many in the impoverished part of the island, followed by confessions for the better part of the day in that village. This evening, you are having dinner with Prime Minister Leese."

"Very well. I look forward to my time with the villagers." Then with a wink he added, "And of course, with the good prime minister." With only a moment's hesitation while again looking out across the water he said, "I do miss being in the home of my predecessors, but the simplicity which this exile affords me—I would not trade it."

Both stood there for a moment, taking in the beauty of the scene. Then Peter spoke again. "We should move to shelter, a storm is brewing."

The monsignor looked out in slight confusion. "But, Holy Father, the sky is clear?"

The Pontiff nodded as he continued to stare out over the ocean.

"Yes, it certainly appears that way, does it not?"

6

"Souls smell in Hades."

– Heraclitus

Vanya walked up the center aisle of Our Lady of the Lake Church, selecting the third pew from the front. She genuflected and then slid in far enough so that one or perhaps even two others could slip in without her having to move. She removed her rosary from her purse, made the sign of the cross, and began to recite the Apostle's Creed to herself. She was having a difficult time concentrating. Her dream of Luther was now haunting her nearly every night, and she had found her paranoia growing to the point where she constantly felt as if eyes were upon her.

Vanya slowly turned her head to the left, spotting only two other people in the entire church. One man, who looked to be at least seventy years old, had his head buried in his clasped hands. He was mumbling to himself, and Vanya soon recognized that he was reciting something in Latin.

The other individual looked like a street woman. Despite the warm weather, she was bundled up and fiddling with a brown paper bag. Vanya allowed a sense of pity to briefly interrupt her feelings of anxiety.

She looked forward and saw that the confessional was no longer occupied. Vanya liked this specific church because it still maintained the older tradition of speaking to the priest through a screen as opposed to face to face. The retired priest, a holy man and one-time personal assistant to a Pope years before, was the eldest brother of Father Craig Ebright, the Diocesan priest from St. Louis who would travel clandestinely to Ephesus to administer the Sacraments to her and the boys. It had been at Father Craig's suggestion that she and Jesse had settled here, in Pergamum.

She slipped into the booth and knelt. Instantly Vanya heard the calming voice of Father Tyler through the screen.

PHOENIX

"In the name of the Father, the Son, and the Holy Spirit. Proceed my child, and may God grant you the ability to provide a good confession."

Vanya responded in her typical rote fashion. "Bless me, Father, for I have sinned. It has been almost a month since my last confession. Since then I—"

"It's been a *long* time, Vanya," the voice asserted.

"Well, it has been a..." she paused, somewhat startled. "Forgive me, Father, what did you say?"

"I said continue on, please," the voice responded.

Vanya was a bit disconcerted. She continued. "Well, since my last confession, I have been dishonest four times, and had inappropriate thoughts on seven occasions, I—"

"I have missed the sweet smell of your fears."

Vanya blinked. She hesitated, a slight touch of trepidation now permeating her consciousness. "Father?"

"Yes, my child?"

"I'm sorry, what did you say?" Vanya questioned timidly.

"I asked how you were invoked into these lies."

She rubbed her temples. *This can't be happening! Not here!*

"You see, Father, it's a bit complicated, but my nephew and I—"

"YOU CANNOT RUN ANYMORE, VANYA! I HAVE GROWN STRONGER!"

The bellowing voice seemed to echo throughout the church. Vanya fell back as a gust of putrid air burst through the screen. A deep laugh reverberated from behind it, growing louder with each round of hysterics.

She grappled for her flask of holy water. But as she pulled it from her purse, the flask sailed from her hands, smashing against the side of the booth. However, instead of holy water splattering, Vanya saw droplets of blood streaming down the wall.

She watched in terror as the droplets of blood trickled upon the floor, sizzling like acid. Her eyes grew wider as she realized the burns in the floor were spelling out a name.

JESSE

ii

Jonathan sat by the edge of the river on the rock he had so enjoyed diving off as a child. The river was no more than five meters below, but as a boy of eleven, it had seemed like a kilometer down.

Every now and then, when the dreams became too real, he would come out to this haven to think and pray. He could just close his eyes, and he would soon be light years away. In this place, which was as real to him as the day, he would be reunited with his brother and the mother he never knew. As he floated off, Jonathan would hear the delicate sounds of his Aunt Vannie's harpsichord.

His mother would gaze upon him with proud, yet concerned eyes. She was more beautiful than any picture had dared attempt to portray. And then she would say those words which always invoked tears of joy in him:

"I Love you, Jesse."

This was paradise. This was what love and life could be. But sadly the image would begin to fade, and as it did, Jesse could swear the pleasant expressions on the faces of his mother and Tobias would fade as well. Was that last glimpse, one of... *fear?*

Fully immersed in his reverie, Jonathan felt himself hurling back towards Earth, feeling vibrations in his ears. Suddenly, the walls of fantasy crumbled down.

"JON!"

Jonathan jerked, realizing there was someone else with him, right next to him in fact. A hand grabbed his shoulder, and for an instant Jonathan felt the sensation of falling.

"Jesus, Jon!"

Jonathan stopped, steadied himself and looked up. There above him, with a look of both concern and confusion, was Nathan.

"You had that stupid look on your face again, man. Where the hell do you go when you're like that?"

Jonathan looked down, a little embarrassed, and not without a twinge of irritation. "What are you doing here, Nate?"

Nathan shrugged. "Well, I was actually thinking about coming out here to end it all, and then I found that you'd beaten me to the punch!"

Jonathan chuckled softly and shook his head, having regathered the majority of his wits. "Always the perennial jokester. Seriously, Nate, what gives?"

Nathan allowed the grin to fade from his face. "I should be asking you that question. Don't think I haven't noticed the fact that you've been avoiding me since... since the accident."

Jonathan turned his head away. "I don't want to talk about it," he mumbled.

"Fine," Nathan shrugged. "Don't make no difference to me. I'd just as soon you didn't throw any religious crap at me about what happened anyway."

Jonathan looked up at Nathan, annoyed. "I've never said a word trying to push my beliefs on you!"

"No, no, you haven't," Nathan agreed. "But you've thought it. I've seen it in your eyes. I also saw all those simple-minded people kneeling before you like you were some god—"

"I'm not!" Jonathan snapped.

"*I* know that," Nathan retorted. "Because I have no problem believing in *you*."

Jonathan sighed deeply and allowed his eyes to survey the opposite shoreline. Nathan's chosen faith of atheism *did* bother him some, but it was his total disrespect for other people's beliefs that made Jonathan downright angry at times. After a brief moment of tension, Nathan took a seat beside Jonathan.

"So what's goin' on in that skull of yours?" he inquired.

Jonathan paused only for a moment. "I've been moving in the wrong direction."

Nathan looked at his friend inquisitively.

Without even so much as a glance, Jonathan continued, "Remember how we used to play around at your house?" he began. "You taught me a little bit of bass guitar, and we'd play songs together?"

Nathan smiled. "Sure. If I remember correctly, you used to put some pretty poetic lyrics to some of that stuff. We didn't exactly have the voices of Simon and Garfunkel, but it wasn't bad."

"No, it wasn't," Jonathan agreed, still looking off into nothingness.

"That experience was so relaxing to me. So *comforting*." Jonathan sighed, allowing his memory to slip back to his early childhood. "I guess music has always been that way for me."

Nathan looked over curiously. He was not sure where his friend was going with this, but he was starting to feel a bit dreamy himself.

"We can always do it again, Jon-boy," Nathan suggested, watching for a response.

Jonathan began to nod, and traces of a pleasant smile began to form on his face. "I'd like that," he whispered.

Nathan smiled and found himself nodding also. He paused briefly, still not quite understanding the gist of the conversation. He finally gave up being sensitive and assumed a more direct approach.

"What's going on, Jon?"

Jonathan hesitated and then turned towards Nathan, staring straight into his eyes. "I'm not going to college."

Nathan stared back, stunned. His response came out in a disbelieving laugh. "Wh-What do you mean?"

"Just what I said," Jonathan responded, nodding his head while biting his lower lip.

"You're serious?"

"Yes, I'm serious."

Nathan looked away in disbelief, shaking his head. "I'll be damned." After a beat, his gaze turned back to Jonathan. "So then, what are you going to do?"

"For now?" Jonathan asked rhetorically, shrugging his shoulders, and then turning towards Nathan with a rapidly erupting grin he said, "I think I'm going to play bass."

iii

Paula Sauerbrey stepped into the church and sat in the back pew, contemplating whether or not this would be the week she would make it into the confessional. She saw only a street woman and an elderly man sitting at different ends of the church. The confessional light seemed to indicate a vacancy.

I'm not so sure about this, maybe I should wait to see if anyone else wants to go.

Suddenly, a door to a nearby closet burst open, and none other than the mother of Jonathan Storm rushed out. She had a look of terror in her eyes, and without even so much as a glance towards the others in the church, she flew out the front doors, muttering and moaning like someone in deep distress.

The door to the priest's confessional opened up, and out stepped the perplexed, retired priest. "What? What is all the commotion?" He glanced over and saw the closet door open. "My heavens, what has happened here?"

Paula was caught off-guard and dipped her head, covering her face with her hands as if in deep prayer. She did not wish the priest to see her.

What is he doing here? I thought he was away...

Father Tyler moved to peer inside the closet; Paula stole a glance back towards the church entrance, though now regarding it as more of an exit.

Maybe... maybe today isn't the day after all...

7

I have a Dark Side.

I know Him by name.

He is creative...
> His art spews forth from buried pain.

He is seductive...
> His lust for flesh knows no bounds.

He is confident...
> For He has nothing to lose.

And He is dangerous...
> For He knows not of his own mortality.

But,
If the truth be known
He is also lonely
He is hurt
He is scared.

He is a part of me
My Personal Demon
And I will not relinquish Him.

For in this world
> I need him

And in the next...
> Please God,
> Forgive Him.

– Jonathan Corban Storm
Duality

PHOENIX

i

"Vanya!"

Dr. Ilyushenko chirped in delight upon seeing his sole patient's guardian. She smiled genuinely as they embraced. Ilyushenko was still beaming as he helped Vanya to a seat in front of his desk. He quickly slid into his own chair.

"It is good to see you, so good," he began, then his facial expression transformed quickly. "I-I was quite devastated to hear of your brother. I pray they are able to find the *sooka* who did this, and that your mother—may God bless her a thousand times—may find some peace in this God-forsaken land."

Vanya's eyes teared up, and she found herself unable to respond.

"Is there anything I can do, Vanya? You know, all you have to do is ask."

"No," Vanya breathed barely louder than a whisper.

Ilyushenko nodded in acknowledgement. "I understand. We do not need to talk of such things now. I suppose we can get to the topic at hand. How are things at home?"

Vanya sighed, but still managed to maintain a trace of a smile. "I don't know, Viktor, just when things seemed to be coming together, everything is starting to fall apart."

Ilyushenko looked steadily at Vanya. "How do you mean?"

She provided a subtle shrug while wiping the moisture from her eyes. "Well, to begin, though he won't exactly admit it, my father is in hiding."

Ilyushenko nodded, as it was clear that this was not unanticipated news. "Yes, I am not surprised. He was made out to be the fall guy in Danny's execution. That is no doubt at the center of this business with Yerik. Truly, the family business, it is not what it used to be."

"I wish it never was."

He took a moment, eyeing Vanya intently, then spoke again. "I am sorry, Vanya. We have stepped upon this ground again. Let us trust that your father will do what is necessary. So please tell me... in the bigger picture, how are things going for you?"

Vanya tried to portray a smile of acknowledgment but ended up looking down to the floor, not having been prepared to deal with her own pain. She returned her gaze to Ilyushenko.

"Viktor, I know you didn't call me in here to ask about me. You're concerned about Jonathan, aren't you?"

Ilyushenko paused, but then nodded slowly as he leaned back in his chair. "Yes, I am," he began. "I realize you have a lot going on... and I was almost hesitant to bring it up at this time."

"Please, just tell me what you want to tell me, Viktor."

Ilyushenko nodded in acknowledgement. "Very well, out with it I suppose. Amongst other things, Jonathan appears to be having some episodes."

"Episodes? What kind of episodes?"

"Psychotic ones."

"What?" she did not like the implications of that phrase.

"It is not what you think, Vanya. I am just saying that there are moments when he just slips out of reality."

"Like when he gets that funny look on his face, and he doesn't respond to me?"

Ilyushenko sat forward, folding his hands on the table. "Yes, that is the way it has been, but last week he told me that he healed an injured girl, and I think he really believes he did it."

Vanya looked curiously at the doctor. "Well," she stated apprehensively, "Jonathan never has been one to make up lies."

Ilyushenko tilted his head, raising one eyebrow. "Well, you know, Vanya, that really brings me to my next concern."

Vanya looked at the doctor curiously.

"What? That he's honest?"

He shook his head. "No, Vanya, not *just* that. What I am thinking, or should I say what I am asking, is has Jonathan *ever* displayed any negative behavior since his brother was killed?"

"What do you mean, Viktor?"

He shrugged. "Has he ever talked back to you? Has he ever gotten into a fight at school, has he ever gotten drunk, or smoked pot, or thrown a temper tantrum?"

Vanya looked astonished. "Why, no, Viktor. Is that such a problem?"

Ilyushenko shook his head. "No, not exactly a problem. It is just that these behaviors would be considered… normal, even healthy in some cases for a teenager." He paused for a moment, following along with Vanya's expressions, then continued. "Are you aware, Vanya, that Jonathan carries a great deal of pain inside of him?"

"Well, I'd imagine he must after all he's been through."

"Yes, Vanya, you are right, it *has* to be there. But except for his occasional expression of feelings of sadness and guilt, I do not see him acting out any of the expected feelings."

"Well, what *do* you expect, Viktor?" Vanya asked, bordering on exasperation.

"Rage," he responded solemnly.

"What?"

"Pure, unadulterated rage, Vanya. I know it is there. I have done numerous projective tests, and it *is* there. And what is more, I would not even say that it is buried. Only that it is *not a part of Jonathan*."

Vanya had reached a stage of utter confusion at this point. "Viktor, this is getting beyond what I understand as common sense. What exactly are you saying?"

Ilyushenko looked off into space, trying to think of how he could explain his thoughts in plain English.

Russian is so much clearer! he thought.

After a moment, he leaned forward.

"Vanya," he began slowly. "Carl Jung long ago described a concept known as 'the self' and its alter ego, 'the shadow'. The 'self' was basically all those positive, and some mildly negative, aspects of our personality which we believe we possess. It is who we think we are—our personal identity. We tend to make decisions based on how we would expect ourselves to decide, using our own self-image. So, it is generally self-perpetuating."

Ilyushenko looked closely at Vanya and, recognizing the expression of comprehension on her face, he continued on.

"The problem arises when the individual has a seemingly 'bad' thought, or perhaps performs an antisocial act. The 'self' usually does not want to assimilate this into its identity. It subconsciously looks for environmental factors to blame. If it cannot find any, it attributes these negative traits to 'the shadow'."

Vanya began to shake her head. "I'm sorry, Viktor, this is starting to sound like psychobabble to me."

Ilyushenko raised his hand and nodded in acknowledgment of Vanya's comment, yet he continued on. "Yes, I know it must, but I am certain of it. Projective testing shows Jonathan to be living in a dichotomous state."

"What?"

Ilyushenko paused. "To 'the shadow', Jonathan has attributed all but a speck of his negative energy. The 'self', the Jonathan we see, is nearly perfect. The shadow, however, is growing and starting to slip into his consciousness. Initially it was through his dreams, but now it is even breaking through in the middle of the day." Ilyushenko again paused, allowing Vanya to assimilate the concepts he was suggesting. "What I fear is the existence of a distinct negative personality which Jonathan has unconsciously developed over the years."

"Are you saying he's schizophrenic?" Vanya yelped.

Ilyushenko incurred a look of concern, or perhaps even dismay on his face. "I would probably suggest a greater likelihood of Jonathan potentially developing a dissociative identity disorder."

Vanya sat back in her seat, utterly shocked. "So what does this mean, Viktor? Is my nephew going to go insane?"

"Not necessarily, Vanya. *If* this shadow is permitted to continue to seep through at a controlled rate, and Jonathan is able to slowly assimilate the negative energy, he can possibly build the bridges to integrate the personalities in a healthy way."

Vanya paused, digesting this thought, then leaned forward. "And if it all bursts forth at once?"

Ilyushenko would not answer this question; it was one he had asked himself on more than a few occasions. His fears were too great to trouble Vanya with at this time.

ii

Samuel Hagarot walked anxiously down the hallway. He had been ecstatic, at first, at the prospect of meeting with the great Luther. His mother had always been so ambiguous in her portrayal of him; at times depicting him as a great man of power and conviction, at other times, seemingly out of nowhere, cursing his name.

She would not have approved of this visit, but it had been years since Samuel had permitted her (or her current husband for that matter) to have dominion over his life. She was an intellectual dwarf—he had been confident of this fact by the age of seven. Discovering that he himself, on the other hand, not only had an intellect far superior than that of his peers, but that creative forces dwelt within him—forces that seemed to be far beyond those that would have been thought possible for a mere man.

His many talents had also proven financially profitable, sparing him the fate of nearly a quarter of the workforce now living off of near-perpetual unemployment. Though many others had responded to the Second Depression by entering into agricultural opportunities, Samuel was grateful that his talents had been discovered early on by men of influence. Yet it was not until recently that he had caught the eye of the one he truly desired affirmation from, Luther.

He had found the boy, Jesse, on his own. Despite his young age, when Samuel had learned of his half-brother's existence (through incessant prodding of his mother), it had become a passion of his—even an obsession—to track him down. There had been another brother as well, Tobias, whom his mother had acknowledged. But somewhere within him, Samuel sensed that this one was no more. Jesse was a different story, however. Samuel found that, though no doubt assisted by the extensive research and investigative work, it was ultimately his intuition that led him to Jesse's location.

And that had brought him here today.

Samuel reached the end of the hallway and stepped into the reception area. Without so much as a glance, the receptionist moved for the intercom. Before she could reach the button, however, Luther's voice came across.

"Send him in, Elizabeth."

She held out a hand, directing Samuel to the only apparent doors in the room, aside from the entrance. He took a deep breath and walked through them.

He was initially struck by the color of the room, or perhaps *lack* of color would be more accurate. The walls, carpet, and even furniture were a dull gray. The chair behind the desk, which had been facing the opposite direction, swung around to reveal a very intense-looking, late middle-aged individual. His eyes soul piercing, Luther held his fingertips touching each other in a contemplative gesture.

Luther did not initially speak but stared at the boy for some time. Perhaps it was not the standard reunion that ordinary people would experience. Then again, this pair was anything but ordinary.

"Well, it is good to finally meet you... *son*."

"And you, Father."

8

"Music was invented to confirm human loneliness."

– Lawrence Durrell

Vanya looked warily about her surroundings before crossing the street towards the Corner Street Café. In a town that had grown quite rundown and in near disrepair (as were most of the towns in the country now), this one café had managed to keep a clean and pleasant appearance. She would expect no less from an establishment owned by her father.

Feeling comfortable that no one was paying much attention to her, she quickly moved across the way and slid in the front door of the café. Vanya glanced about the interior and quickly recognized the back of the figure she was seeking. The tension in her muscles eased just a little as she moved towards the man. She gracefully slid into the booth, opposite her guest.

Though they knew to keep their voices down, the expressions on their faces could hardly have been described as discreet.

"Vanya! Oh, it is so good to see you!"

"Papa, my heavens, how long has it been?"

"Three years, four months, and six days since our last rendezvous. But who is keeping track? You are looking beautiful. Like a rose in the desert, though I may never get used to that new nose of yours... so... so not like a girl from the motherland."

Vanya blushed. Her father could still do that to her. However, her face quickly grew graver.

"How bad are things, Papa?"

Nesterov chuckled. "My daughter Vanya, always getting down to business. Things are not so good, but they are not so horrible either. I have a dozen men or so with me. I am looking at relocating to southeastern Virginia. The organizations there are relatively weak, and I would not be so far from you."

"So," Vanya began, somewhat cautiously, "is there any chance that you can make peace with the remainder of the Caputo family?"

Nesterov sighed. "Sure. I can get back in their good graces and complete a personal vendetta all in one pop."

Vanya looked suspiciously at her father. "How's that?"

"Easy," Nesterov responded. "Whack—I really love that American term—Harold Freeman and his entire family."

"Father!" Vanya interjected.

"Do not be upset, Vanya. This is the real world. I did not choose to be in this situation. I must do what I must. In this, now, there is no choice."

"There is always a choice, Father."

Nesterov paused. This line of discussion was no use. He wanted to speak, wanted to tell Vanya everything. But after what had happened to Yerik, well, less information was best. He quickly changed the subject.

"How is Jes—ah, forgive me—Jonathan doing?" he asked.

Vanya shrugged, also somewhat grateful about the change of subject. "Okay, I suppose." She was lying, and sensed that her father was aware of this. "Oh, he's had a few problems recently, and old Viktor gave me a bit of a scare with his psycho-garbage, but I'd say he's managing all right. I think he's just going through a bit of a phase."

Nesterov had a puzzled look on his face. "How so?"

Vanya sighed. "Well, about a month or so ago he sat me down and gave me that 'I need to find myself' speech. Says he's not going to college just yet. Seems that he's spending all his time playing music with his friend Nathan."

Nesterov raised an eyebrow. "Music, you say? I remember not too long ago I had a hell of a time pulling a young lady away from the harpsichord I had bought for her. And if I remember correctly, you gave up many activities, saying that you would one day play Bach in Carnegie Hall."

Vanya produced a slightly saddened smile. She dwelt on the harpsichord she had left behind in Jeffrey's house at times, certain that it had been destroyed in the fire. She glanced out the window, just for an instant, and for a moment she thought she recognized Carol Lindsey, Nathan's aunt, scurrying down the street. The woman looked back once, appearing somewhat distressed. Vanya was puzzled and had to restrain the instinct to call out to her.

"What is it, Vanya?" Nesterov inquired.

Vanya snapped out of her brief reverie. "I'm sorry, Papa. I forgot myself. I thought I saw a friend of mine."

She sat and contemplated for another moment, then spoke up again. "Where do we stand with Luther, Papa?"

Nesterov shrugged his shoulders. "I know I am usually the one who says you cannot be too careful, but I honestly think he has given up. We stopped tracking him about six months ago when things started getting hairy within the syndicate. He was spending all his time trying to unite all these satanic-type groups under himself. I believe he has succeeded too. Much silliness! What is interesting is that now there has been this big unification, they no longer seem to be engaging in any insane practices like before, like with…" Nesterov trailed off as his eyes began to tear up for a moment. "Anyway, they are far less public. Still, I have no indication that he is still looking—at least not with any significant effort that I can see. I believe he has moved on."

Vanya had ceased to respond facially to what her father was saying. Nesterov noticed this and lowered his tone to one of concern.

"You are still having these dreams?" he asked.

Vanya nodded.

Nesterov hesitated for a moment as Vanya became teary eyed. "And Jes—Jonathan?"

Vanya cleared her throat as a tear fell down her cheek. "A few weeks back, I woke up and found Jonathan standing over me with a knife in his hand. It wasn't raised or anything, but he had an awful look in his eyes. He snapped out of it pretty quickly when I screamed, and then he cried for the rest of the night. I just don't know, Papa."

Nesterov looked alarmed. "Vanya, you must get that boy back to Viktor!"

ii

Carol Lindsey did not slow her pace until she reached the Walnut Community Organization office, where her husband worked. She shot up the stairs and into the office. The secretary recognized her instantly.

"Well hello, Mrs. Lindsey. How are you to—?"

"I need to see to Har— ahh— Jack, now!" Carol blurted out.

The secretary, an excitable man, jumped up. "What's wrong?"

Carol did not have time to waste, however, and moved past the secretary down the hall.

The secretary's voice called out from behind her. "He's in the conference room with a customer, if you wait just a moment I can—"

Carol burst into the conference room. Several men sitting around a table quickly turned their heads toward her. Jack, her husband, stood up immediately.

"Carol?" There was a moment's pause as Jack Lindsey looked at his associates uncomfortably. He then looked back to his wife, witnessing her anxious expression. "What's wrong?" he asked.

"I need to speak with you, Jack, right away."

Jack nodded to her and politely excused himself from the conference. He took Carol by the arm and led her down the hall and into his own office. She was sobbing by this point. Jack closed the door, and Carol instantly embraced him.

"Easy, honey, easy. What's going on?"

"I saw him, I saw Nesterov!" she managed to blurt out between sobs.

Jack momentarily pulled himself away, still holding Carol by the shoulders. His expression had transformed to one of deep concern.

"You *what?*" he responded, knowing perfectly well what she had said yet still needing a moment to absorb the ramifications of her statement.

Carol began to ease up on her sobbing, now having someone to share her concern. "I saw Alexandre Nesterov at the Corner Street Café with Vannie Storm!"

Jack detached himself, staring off into nothingness with a look of confusion on his face. He sat down at his desk. "Are you sure?"

PHOENIX

Carol looked hurt. "Of course I'm sure. Don't you think I've had his face engraved in my mind, looking for him around every corner? It was him, Jack. It was *him*!"

Jack continued to stare off into space as the first drop of sweat dripped down his left temple. "Did they see you?"

Carol sat down opposite her husband. "I think Vannie might have, but by that time my back was to Nesterov."

Jack began to shake his head absently. He again looked at his wife. "Vannie?"

"Yes, Vannie!" Carol interjected defensively.

He wiped his brow and reflected for a moment. Thoughts began to run through his head. Nesterov with *Vannie?* She had always seemed to have a slight familiarity about her, though he could never put his finger on it. Nesterov had always kept him at arm's length (so long as your arm was the length of a city block), excepting for that one time he had gone on assignment with the old man's son Yerik to check in on—

The blood drained from his face.

Vanya?

He had really only seen her once—Nesterov's daughter—and that was a brief glance primarily of the back of her head in a remote diner in the Midwest. But this woman, Vannie Storm, didn't resemble her, or at least what he remembered of her, in the slightest... or did she? No doubt, Vanya could have easily taken the same path as he; it was amazing what plastic surgery—and in his case a beard—could do.

"What are you thinking, Harold? What just crossed your mind?" Carol's anxiety was beginning to cycle up again.

Then again, this was ludicrous; the Storms had been here for years *before* they themselves had arrived. So if it *were* the Nesterovs, and they knew he was there, what would they be waiting for?

"Harold! I'm talking to you!"

He took a deep breath and then looked up towards his wife. She must be mistaken, but in these times he could not take a chance. "This doesn't add up, Vio—I mean Carol, but we can't go back home. Go ahead and text Nathan. Put the code in, and we'll all meet at the designated area in one hour. We're okay as long as we keep our heads."

iii

"That's a take!"

Jonathan laughed as he put down the bass guitar, switching off the amplifier. "Do you think we're ready for the big time?"

"Yeah, right," Nathan responded, flipping the 'off' switch to his digital recorder.

Jonathan followed Nathan with his eyes. "You know, Nate, we could probably make a few bucks to give to a good cause, with so many people out of work and all." He looked hesitantly, trying to read Nathan's face. "Why don't we try to do some gigs in Wilmington, or maybe even Durham or Raleigh?"

Nathan chuckled, shaking his head as he put his guitar in its case. "Jon, please give it up. It's not going to happen."

Jonathan looked hurt. "Why not? The couple of songs we wrote sound pretty good, don't you think?"

Nathan reluctantly nodded. "Yeah, *real* good in fact. And your voice is very distinctive. But this is just for fun, Jon-boy. You got a bright future ahead of you. The final cut-off for late entrance is next week, and you're going to college, buddy. No ifs, ands, or buts!"

Jonathan shook his head, lying back on the couch. "I'm not going, Nate. I really can't say exactly why, but I just know it's not for me right now."

Nathan continued to shake his head as he put away his patch cords. Jonathan, not one to be easily swayed, sat up and began to speak in a more conciliatory tone.

"How about this, Nate. My scholarship can be delayed a year. I already checked it out. We can give it a shot, for one year, and if we don't show any promise by that point, I'm off to Kent State, no complaints. What do you say?"

Nathan looked at Jonathan, exasperated. "This is so unlike you, Jon. Part of me, okay, a *big* part, wants to say 'let's go for it', but it's a million to one shot. So few recording labels left, very little access for the average Joe through the Internet market; someone who's got other options should—"

Just then Nathan's cell phone buzzed, cutting off the discussion instantly. Jonathan was about to resume the debate when he noticed the dramatic change in Nathan's countenance as he looked down at his text message.

PHOENIX

"What's wrong, Nate?" he inquired.

Nathan did not look back at him. "I've gotta go," he responded before shooting down the stairs and out the door.

A New Kind Of Goodfella?

Excerpted from NewsWatch Magazine

The execution of Danny Caputo, the leading mob figure in North America, was more than the end of an evil man. It was the end of an era.

It is hard not to look back on the early days of the Italian mafia without a sense of nostalgia. Days where loyalty rested solely on family ties, not on the almighty dollar. Days where a sense of honor, though perhaps misguided, prevented nationwide battles that caused ongoing strife and killings. All wise-guys knew which was *their* turf and which was not.

Gone are those days. Where families once ruled, syndicates now reign. And despite the weakness of internal law enforcement over the past decade, a resurgence in crime fighting (a la President Hugh Jennings Lang) has begun. Due to the advancement of policing and surveillance technologies, one will soon have to be a computer programmer to commit a crime in the United States. So what has happened? Have all organized criminals turned in their Tommy guns for *iBerry's*?

Nope. There's a new name to the game. Diversification. Globalization. The Russian mafia found a home in the U.S. Why? Because "business as usual" had become nearly impossible in this country and many "old-style" Mafioso would not or could not change their stripes. However, through this new partnership, forged by Mr. Caputo himself, U.S. organized crime leaders could co-manage their same game with the Russian mobsters, who still control over 50% of all Russian commercial enterprises abroad.

A "match made in hell?" Well, despite all else, Caputo was able to keep the delicate peace – a peace whose end was signaled by the recent slaying of Yerik Nesterov, son of the elusive Alexandre Nesterov, right-hand man of the late Caputo.

So let's be real, folks. As long as greed continues to be a corrupting force in our public officials, there will always be work for those neo-mobsters who know how far a buck and a pistol can get you.

Hmmm… it seems the more things change, the more they stay the same.

PHOENIX

i

Nathan sprinted the last leg towards the Seventh Heaven Motel and burst through the front entrance. He was well out of breath, never having been the athletic type. The clerk, alarmed by Nathan's abrupt entrance, jumped back and ducked behind the counter.

"Please, sir, the money is in the register. Please don't kill me!"

Nathan bent over, supporting himself on his knees while he tried to regain his breath. He stood up, still gasping, and moved towards the desk where the clerk had now backed into a corner with his hands raised.

"Please, sir, I have kids, I—"

"Can it, Hoshimoto," Nathan responded, straining to allow sufficient air into his lungs. "I need the room number for Dr. Richard Kimble."

The clerk looked at Nathan curiously and let out a deep sigh of relief. "Oh, excuse me, sir. I am sorry. We have a problem with delinquents here. We—"

"The room number, dickhead!" Nathan repeated insistently.

The clerk nodded. "Of course, sir. Just arrived here a few minutes ago. Room 23. Will you be stay—?"

But Nathan had already run out the door. He arrived at the motel room door not thirty seconds later. He knocked in the manner that he had been instructed to do in this situation since the age of twelve, the Morse code for "S.O.S."

The door opened, and Nathan slid into the room. He saw his father standing in the entrance, his mother sitting on the edge of the bed. They both looked gravely troubled. His mother got up and hugged him.

After a brief moment passed, Nathan spoke. "What's going on?" he asked, releasing his mother.

His parents exchanged looks, then his father began to speak. "Your aunt—aww hell—your *mom* thinks she just saw Alexandre Nesterov in town a few hours ago."

"What? How?" Nathan was having a difficult time assimilating this information. "Are you sure? I mean, did you get any warning from the Bureau?"

"No," his father responded. "But they're on their way here right now to relocate us. I've got your—"

"What?" Nathan responded disbelievingly. "Relocate? No, no wait a minute! You said we were done… that this one was the last. I'm sick of all of this, Dad!" He looked desperately towards his mother. "I can't. I've got friends here… I finally have a life of my own!"

Nathan's father placed a reassuring hand on his son's shoulder, and the two sat down on the edge of the bed. A thousand thoughts and scenarios ran through Nathan's head.

"Nathan, think about this for a minute. It's not safe here anymore. We can't stay."

But Nathan shook his head defiantly. "No, that's not altogether true, it's not safe for *you*. We've got different last names. I-I can stay with Jon. The Bureau can arrange an accident. The—"

"It's Jonathan's mother who Nesterov was with!" his mother blurted out, bursting into tears.

Nathan looked towards his father for confirmation of this fact. His father nodded, following it with a slight shrug. Nathan's eyes widened in disbelief as he moved over to the opposite side of the bed, placing his head in his hands. He was trying desperately to absorb all the information that had just been presented to him. After several minutes of reflection, Nathan spoke in a monotone voice.

"I'm not going."

His mother looked towards him, terrified. She turned to her husband. "For God's sake, Harold, talk some sense into him!"

Nathan shook his head. "No. I've made up my mind. I'm tired of this running around. I'm tired of getting a new identity every few years. I don't want to start over. This is *not* my battle. I've done my time, and I'm not going."

"Son," his father started, but now seemingly halfheartedly. "We've got to stick together. We… we're all each other has. If we separate now, who knows when we'll be able to see each other again?"

"I'm aware of that, Dad," Nathan responded. Then, with a calm but assured voice he stated, "But I'm staying."

Harold Freeman released a painful sigh. He had feared this day would come, when the family would go their separate ways. He could not argue his son's point—Nathan was right. This was not his battle. He had not asked for this life. Harold looked back towards his wife, who returned his gaze with terrified eyes, anxiously awaiting his rectification of the situation.

"Okay," he replied.

Carol, a.k.a. Violet Freeman, gasped. "Harold! We can't leave him behind!"

"We can't force him to go." Harold moved over and sat down at the desk. He thought for a minute and then spoke to Nathan. "You can't live with Jonathan though, Nathan. Though I can't fully get my mind around how, for all we know, he might be a part of this. You'll have to lay low for a while—a good long while—and hopefully Nesterov will split town, believing we've all left."

Nathan looked at his father as tears began to well up in his eyes.

His father continued. "I don't like this one bit, Nathan. It's risky, it's dangerous."

Nathan slowly nodded. "I can stay with Simon, Dad. Outside of town. Jonathan doesn't know him. I'll hang low until I get the word it's okay to come out. Okay?"

Nathan looked over at his mother, who was now sobbing quietly. "Mom, it'll be okay. It... it could be just a coincidence Nesterov's here. We'll work it out. We always do—"

"You'd better go, Nathan," Harold Freeman interrupted, which struck Nathan as somewhat cold.

Nathan looked towards his father, startled by the tone of his voice. This was really going to be it. He nodded and hugged his mom. Nathan turned his gaze towards his father across the room. He held up a hand to wave, then slipped out the door.

Violet was able to get out one last comment in between sobs before her Valium began to settle in.

"We're never going to see him again..."

ii

Jonathan walked back towards his home through Goodman Forest a few hours after nightfall. He strolled dreamily along the trail that the young Jonathan and Nathan had carved out years back. The trees, starting to brown early this year, were swaying heavily, and Jonathan began to feel a touch of vertigo.

He looked up the path and saw an orange hue begin to break through the darkness. Uncomfortable thoughts from the past began to slide into his consciousness as he approached an unfamiliar clearing in the woods. His feet began to tingle, and suddenly he felt a burst of energy seemingly propel him upwards. He sensed that he reached an apex, then for an instant Jonathan felt as if he were falling. His eyes blurred, then slowly came back into focus. Directly in front of him stood a looming figure out of his past.

"Do you know me, Jesse?" The all-too-familiar voice called out.

Jesse realized he was now standing on a plateau high above the rest of the Earth. A warm breeze gently swept through his hair as he looked down upon the nations of the world. The scene had a surreal feel to it, but Jesse knew this was not a dream.

"I know who you are," Jesse responded, feeling a twinge of anger seep into his voice.

A strangely warm smile broke out across Luther's face. *"It is so good to see you again, my son."*

"Don't call me that!" Jesse's anger was clearly evident now. In his dreams, Luther had referred to him in this manner. But when he had questioned his Aunt Vannie about it, she had simply told him that his father was a good man who had tried with all his might to get his mother to leave Jeffrey. She claimed he had disappeared soon afterward.

"Very well," Luther conceded, turning away from Jesse and looking to the Earth below. *"I have sensed that others have attempted to turn you against me, Jesse. I have been away a long time—that is regrettable."*

"Regrettable?" Jesse yelped. *"Turned against you? You killed my brother! You meant to kill me! No one had to turn me. You allowed me to hate you just fine yourself!"*

Luther turned partially towards Jesse, feigning a wince. He looked down, completed his turn, and glanced back towards the boy. Jesse was caught off-guard as he saw a troubled look upon Luther's face. A *weakened* look. Luther stepped back and sat on a mid-sized rock nearby. Maintaining an expression of deep concern, Luther began to speak in a much softer tone.

"I understand how you feel. I am sure your childhood is very difficult for you to accurately remember. Especially with that demented doctor twisting all your memories for his own purposes."

Luther looked up again to Jesse and made a gesture towards an adjacent rock a couple of meters from where he was sitting. *"Please, Jesse, rest your weary legs."*

"No, thank you," Jesse responded, trying to sustain his anger. However, he was starting to sense a different feeling seeping into the outskirts of his consciousness. A feeling he did not want to allow to emerge at this moment. A feeling of... *compassion?*

"Your thoughts... they are...incongruent... with your words, my son."

"Don't call me—"

"I am sorry, and I understand that this may be confusing for you, but I can sense the struggle within you. A struggle which is taking place because you know what I am saying to be true."

Jesse felt hot tears begin to form in his eyes, yet he said nothing.

Luther continued, *"You are still wondering how you came upon the power with which you healed that little girl, are you not?"*

Jesse looked up, stunned, as he felt the first tear escape from his eyelid. He absently began to gravitate towards Luther's resting place. *"Y-Yes."*

"That is the gift I passed on to you as a boy. A gift which I can help you develop. Think of the possibilities, Jesse! How you can serve humankind!"

The tears of confusion were now beginning to stream down Jesse's cheeks. He tried to respond. *"I—"*

"No need to say it, son," Luther responded. *"Not just yet. But I will be back. I am here to help, Jesse. Because, though you have had many lies planted into your head, it is important that you know who I am!"*

Jesse stopped in his tracks, now sensing the inevitable words which were about to flow from Luther's lips. Words which he could not bear to hear.

"Yes, Jesse," Luther responded, as if he had read his mind. *"It is true. I am your father."*

"No..." Jesse choked out between his tears as he began to back away.

"Please no..."

"Search your inner heart, Jesse. You know *it to be true. This is who you are, Jesse. You cannot turn your back on your birthright!"*

Jesse clenched his hands against his ears, unable to handle any more of what was being said. He screamed out a resounding *"NO!"* but as the vision began to pale, he heard the voice of Luther fading into the wind.

"I will wait for you, my son..."

iii

Ibn Fatimah was led into a room adorned with many tapestries and items from the glorious history of the Islamic faith. He was directed to a seat at the center of the room. A moment later, another door opened, and in stepped a man, calling out:

"Here enters Caliph Ali Bakr, *al-Muntazar, al-Madhi, al-Mustatir.* May peace be upon him!"

Ibn rose from his seat as the larger than life persona of Caliph Ali Bakr, the promised "Hidden Imam" entered the room.

"Asalamu aleykum," Ibn offered with a slight bow of his head.

"Wa aleykum us sallaam," Ali Bakr responded.

With the brief Islamic greeting exchanged, the two sat down facing each other. A subsequent hand gesture of the Caliph cleared the room of the remaining men.

They sat for a moment in silence before the Caliph began to speak.

"It is good that we are able to finally meet alone."

"It is an honor, Teacher," the much younger Ibn responded. "I must admit that it has been quite a curiosity that you wished to meet with someone of my meager stature and age."

The Caliph raised his hand and shook his head. "You should know, I do not judge by appearances but by the will of Allah. And it is for this reason that I have asked you here today."

Ibn bowed his head in acknowledgement. For many, it would be excessively intimidating to sit before the man (if he could be called that) who in a mere seven years had united the Islamic nations and seemingly healed all Muslim divisions. Quite amazingly, the vast majority of Europe had fallen in less than a month through the well-orchestrated (by man or Allah, it was still contested) grassroots insurgence of the thriving Muslim population within the continent. Initiated via the coordinated and simultaneous detonation of eleven nuclear devices at targeted parliamentary buildings in the European countries, the fate of all but a handful of European nations was quickly sealed. Coincidentally, or by Muslim interpretation, *providentially*, at that time the leaders of all of these republics had been meeting in Brussels to discuss "the Islamic question" and were summarily assassinated by a once-believed moderate Muslim cleric—a man invited to encourage peace among the multitudes but instead releasing a biological agent that killed all in attendance within minutes.

Only the Prime Minister of Great Britain, Sir Thomas Louis Leese, was absent from this meeting of the heads of states of the once powerful European Union. Having to attend the funeral of his sister and brother-in-law, he had sent an envoy in his place. Within the week, an attempt on the prime minister's life had left him wheelchair bound, but his resolve against the aggressors remained intact.

With the vast majority of Europe already fallen only weeks later, Ali Bakr had ordered a surreptitious invasion of Great Britain. With over a million Islamic militants moving through the thought to be cordoned-off Channel Tunnel, Prime Minister Leese made the difficult decision to blow a hole through a portion of the tunnel, sending every invading Islamic soldier to a watery grave. Threats of incursions from Portugal, Poland, and Russia "encouraged" the intended Islamic air support for this invasion to pull back. A week later, the "Eurabic-Old Europe Non-Aggression Accord" was grudgingly signed by all sides. It was here that Ibn had first met the promised Imam.

"I have called you because I am very aware of the role you played in the signing of the Accord," Ali Bakr offered.

"I was there only in assistance of Mahomet Qutb."

"Your mentor?"

"Yes."

The Caliph nodded. "Yes, the notorious voice of moderation in the Islamic world."

Ibn's eyes narrowed. "I would say the voice of *reason*, with all due respect, Teacher."

It would have seemed that this potential insult might have drawn a reaction from the Caliph. It did not.

"It is a shame, truly, his unfortunate demise."

Ibn looked squarely at the man whom he knew was responsible for the death of his mentor, and was more and more certain intended to have him put to death as well. In his brief thirty years, Ibn had seen much bloodshed—much *unnecessary* bloodshed in his own estimation. It did not line up with his understanding of his Sufi Islamic faith.

"Yes, it was unfortunate," Ibn responded. "Teacher, should I expect the same fate?"

This response did cause hesitation in the otherwise consistently serene Imam. A slight smile emerged from his face.

"You were not in support of the Revolution?"

"I do not believe it was necessary. European society was contracepting itself out of existence. In their arrogance, they were killing any sense of a need for an Almighty Sovereign. In a generation, Europe would have been the uncontested dominion of Allah without ever raising a sword." Ibn was resolute, yet respectful.

"Yet Allah saw fit to seize the day, and it is now ours, without delay."

"Respectfully, Teacher, I believe our hastiness is the reason for the Christian Insurgence. We have transformed the lukewarm into martyrs."

"We allow them to unite and rise up, so that they may be crushed together, crushed...*now*. We have truly become a united Islamic people! We have decimated the atheists!"

"And yet the People of the Book have been handled no differently than these non-believers. For centuries, in our own lands, we were able to coexist! Belief must not be compulsory!"

Ali Bakr smiled subtly, then moved the conversation in a different direction. "Do you not believe that I am the legitimate successor of Mohammed, may peace be upon him, and rightful leader of the Islamic faith?"

Ibn gazed curiously at the Caliph for several moments, then shrugged and nodded. "You have made your case for succession, Teacher. An impeccable pedigree, to be certain. I have no grounds on which to question your identity or your office."

"Does your heart belong to Allah?"

"Without reservation. I believe Islam is the answer."

PHOENIX

This obviously pleased Imam Ali Bakr. "Very well said, young student. Then I believe we shall have no difficulty in working together."

This time it was Ibn who was caught off-guard. "I do not believe I understand."

"The world is full of infidels who do not respect our faith, young Ibn. They respect only those who think and talk as they do. You are seen as a voice of moderation—the *new* voice of moderation. For this reason, I have chosen you to be the Foreign Minister of the Islamic Union."

Ibn was astonished. "But I am... I am too young!"

"Well said, young Ibn. Yet it is not my will, but the will of Allah!"

10

I am like shattered glass
Cutting those who touch me
I have been broken
I am hard and sharp
People can see through me.
They know I can hurt them
I am never confronted
I am always walked around.

– Lori Gauntlet

i

Nathan lay on the couch, practicing finger exercises on his guitar while wrestling with a difficult problem in his head. It had been five weeks since his parents had left, and as he had expected, nothing serious had happened.

The Bureau had contacted him earlier that week, informing him that his family was doing just fine, and that Nesterov was now located somewhere in southeastern Virginia. This had not been the first time his mother had overreacted and the family had to relocate.

And in reality, it just did not make any sense to him. If Jonathan and his mother were spies within the Caputo family, why had they not hit his family years ago? Why didn't they do something before Caputo was executed? What was more, the Storms lived in Pergamum *before* he and his family moved there. No, Nathan was pretty sure that his mother either saw someone who looked a lot like Nesterov with Vannie Storm, or she saw someone that looked like Ms. Storm with Nesterov. Nesterov *was* living only a few hours from the area, so it was not inconceivable that it had been a coincidence.

In any case, however, Nathan still found himself having a hard time picking up the phone and calling Jonathan. Though he thought he had completely convinced himself that this was a false alarm, there was a part of him, a minuscule part, which suggested he was asking for trouble if he reunited with his friend.

He shook his head. "Screw it," he mumbled to himself.

"What was that?" Simon Wilson had just walked into the room, sucking down a container of tonic water, his usual vice. Simon was one of those deep thinkers, heavily into philosophy, with long blond hair and wire-rim glasses. Nathan had always chuckled at the fact that this soft-spoken philosopher and renaissance musician would also get his hands greasy every day as an auto mechanic. Not a bad profession to be in as the days of a disposable society had long gone. Many people were looking to get some extra mileage out of their vehicles, and Simon's uncle, Garfield, ran a fairly successful auto repair business.

Nathan was startled by his unexpected entry. "What? Oh, I was just thinking."

Simon plopped down on the couch. "Well, for you, Nathan, that's ground-breaking material."

He turned on the radio to a classical station and lay back, serenely digesting the notes which filled the air. Getting used to Simon's musical taste would take some time for Nathan.

"Gotta love the FM radio waves being back in use!" Simon smiled, then looked to Nathan. "So when are you going to let me in on who you're hiding from. Paula's parents perhaps?"

Nathan smiled to himself, without answering, and Simon sensed that he would not have his question answered today. He casually changed the subject.

"You know," he began, his eyes shifting from the ceiling to Nathan's face. "I've been listening to one of your music discs. I'm pretty sure it's a demo of some sort. Just guitar, bass, a cheap drum machine and two voices. It wasn't the type of music I'd expect a headbanger like you to be carrying around."

Nathan smiled, absorbing Simon's unwitting complement. "Well, I guess it'd just rock your world to find out that that is me playing and doing backup vocals on that disc."

Simon looked astonished. "No, sir! No way!"

Nathan nodded, even more flattered by Simon's response. "*Way*... a few months ago, I was writing music with a friend of mine, Jonathan." Nathan paused for a moment, reflecting. "You know, I don't remember him having any background in music, except for singing in the school chorus, anyway, we got together and put this stuff out."

Simon sat up in his couch, obviously trying to sort out a number of different thoughts flying through his head. He looked at Nathan curiously. "Would you mind if I played around with it a bit? You know, maybe put down some light keyboard tracks?"

Nathan shrugged. "Sure, I guess. Even though Jonathan might have wanted to, I have no plans on going anywhere with that music anyway."

There was suddenly a crash outside, and then a hard thud against Simon's front door. Simon shook his head in disgust, walked to the front door and opened it. There at his feet lay a large rock. He looked out across the way to watch several kids, probably in their mid-teens, dart through the woods, laughing and hollering.

"Dang kids," he mumbled, then shut the door.

Nathan seemed astonished by Simon's apathetic attitude. "What's that all about?"

Simon closed the door and shrugged. "Just some kids from some other neighborhood. I really don't get what they want."

"What they want? To be assholes, obviously!"

But Simon only shook his head. "No, I don't think so. I found one kid in here a few weeks ago going through my musical equipment. I tried to talk to him, but he just bolted. Ever since, I get rocks thrown at my house every few days. I'm not one to promote the drug-scene anymore, but I wish the dudes would split a Quaalude or two."

"I think a good ass-kicking would do them better."

Simon chuckled and then plopped back down on the couch. "Probably not the best thing for me to have this musical equipment here... not all of us can afford a security guard, rich boy." Simon winked then looked at Nathan inquisitively. "So when do I to get to meet your partner in crime?"

Nathan continued to lie there, contemplating the question to himself. At this point he realized he could not come up with any logical reason as to why he couldn't... *shouldn't* contact Jonathan. The Nesterov situation was a bust; it was over. Nathan had to start getting things going again.

He looked up to Simon and responded, "Sometime this week."

PHOENIX

ii

President Hugh Jennings Lang, along with the Independence Party leader, Senator William Maison (the *loyal* opposition), stood up from the photo-op-friendly-chat session and moved to a secured room in the back of the Philadelphia Convention Center. Their respective entourages followed closely behind.

They had just wrapped up the multi-party "brainstorming" meeting with the Concilium on Foreign Affairs. President Lang, not surprisingly, found himself alone on the differing side of just about every issue and initiative that had been laid on the table. Yet he did so with such wit, intelligence, and savvy that most members were barely able to recognize that not one iota of their agenda was moved forward. Most members, but not Senator Maison.

As Lang and his entourage began to sit down on the far side of the large conference table, Maison cut in, "Are all these people necessary?"

Lang looked up, permitted a slight smile (he did not want it to be obvious that he actually relished Maison's palpable frustration), shrugged his shoulders and nodded. "No, as a matter of fact, no one else is needed." Lang nodded to his own people, who were visibly disappointed (they knew sparks were about to fly) but exited the room in proper subordination. Maison did not require so much as a glance for his own people—they exited immediately.

Both men got comfortable in the now empty room, and the moment the door closed, Maison started in.

"What the hell was that out there?"

Lang could not help but smile this time. "Well, it's good to see you too, William. And perhaps you can be more specific?"

"You know damn well what I am talking about! I can't tell if you're naïve or just plain stupid; you can't do what you are doing. You are about to unravel things that have taken us decades to get in place—"

"Perhaps," Lang interrupted, "you can be more precise on who '*us*' is? Because it seems to me if '*us*' is your party, you only had the Office of the President for two terms, hardly decades. But perhaps you are suggesting you were lockstep with the Liberal Party for the three terms before that? Or are you referring to a different, perhaps *non-elected* 'us'?"

Maison held back momentarily. Despite the fact that he desired to rip this man's throat out, he recognized this line of intimidation was going to get nowhere fast. He quickly adjusted his tone.

"Listen, Hugh… it… it's just very confusing for me, and the rest of the American people as well. You were with us ten years ago—for Heaven's sake, you were Warburg's vice-president for his first term, before you bailed on us."

"Bailed on you?" Lang had to work hard to suppress a laugh. "An interesting take on the situation. The Independence Party was only a few years old—and it publicly promoted the 'New Independence' twelve-year plan. I agreed at the time with the policies; close the borders, nationalize the big companies, reduce foreign trade by 90%, and close down all foreign military bases. We acknowledged it would put us back two generations in prosperity— we knew we'd be functioning like a third-world country for a period of time, but considering the threat and our need for self-preservation, we had little choice—or at least, so I felt at the time."

Senator Maison looked curiously at the president. "Then why, Hugh, did you change?"

Lang shook his head. He was not going to pretend this meeting was anything other than what it was. "I feel as if I am in a game of chess right now, William. No, better than that—poker. I suppose we can continue on, acting as if we each don't know what's in the other's hand, even though it seems like the deck has been stacked." Maison did not budge, and a moment later, Lang let out a sigh. "But very well, this is how we communicate." Lang leaned forward. "To answer your question, no, William, it was not me who changed. And you know what? I don't necessarily know that the party changed either. The reality is that, the more I saw, the more I dug into things, I found that despite the public twelve-year plan, meant be to be for temporary stabilization and protection, there was a different—even contradicting—*private* plan in the works. I have to say, I still don't understand why… it was quite a paradox… moving forward on one agenda privately while publicly promoting what appeared to be the exact opposite. You see, I believed, and continue to believe, in the strict national sovereignty of the United States."

"So does the Independence Party, Mr. President."

"Does it?"

At this point, Hugh Lang was staring straight into the eyes of Maison. *How many of my cards do I want to put out on the table at this point?* the president thought.

It was Senator Maison who broke the silence. "In a brief eighteen months, you have filled your Cabinet with rookies—people who have no business being there. You have begun to reach out to other countries: Russia, Poland, Britain, Portugal, to name just a few. This is *not* part of the New Independence Plan, and definitely not part of the Independence Act. We were to be totally independent of *all* nations within three years of now."

What Maison said was true. Lang had deliberately filled his Cabinet with people outside of the normal "farm team"; not one from the Triune Commission, not one associated with the Rockberger group, and definitely not one with the Concilium on Foreign Affairs. As for the New Independence Act of the United States of America, the promotion of this piece of legislation, which began near the middle of his first term as vice president, was the final straw. Lang now recognized it for what it was: a reactionary isolationist plan that would ultimately sink the United States. Their prior initiatives towards seclusion were necessary in the immediate aftermath of the Philadelphia dirty bomb incident and the subsequent—perhaps even coordinated—cutting off of the foreign oil by the OPEC nations. But the New Independence Act, signed into law six years later, played on fear and went much further than the twelve-year plan had ever proposed.

Yes, there were unintended—though not necessarily unforeseen—consequences to their earlier decisions. The pullout of all U.S. military around the world, in the name of protecting the 'homeland', provided a vacuum which allowed the advancement of communism in sub-Saharan Africa, Central and South America, and all of Southeast Asia, as well as permitting the fall of Europe to Islam. Lang would have to carry this burden to his grave. But perhaps the biggest reason he opted out, eventually becoming the primary nemesis of the Independence Party, was when he learned of the suppression of two means which would have eliminated any threat posed by OPEC.

First, Lang learned that the crude oil and natural gas reserves in the ANWR region were discovered to be more than three hundred times what had been previously thought. Second, a breakthrough in the hydrogen engine had been achieved. This innovative technology made it possible to power the vehicles of the entire world on *any* form of water, with efficiency ratings beyond anything anyone could have dreamed and with zero harmful emissions; yet the program was immediately and silently scrapped when the Independence Party took power. These discoveries were secretly concealed and even halted by powers within the party for reasons that were beyond Lang's comprehension. He quietly left the party (as quietly as a vice president could), and then slowly began to publicly question the party on a number of different policies, not yet ready to fully expose what he knew. Somehow he sensed, until he was in a better place of power, it would be best to keep his thoughts to himself.

Fortunately for him, the American citizens who initially stated they were willing to sacrifice over a twelve-year period for "the good of the nation" had grown weary of living as a third-world country. His promise of a better plan resonated well, and by a narrow margin Lang was elected president as an independent candidate—independent of even the Independence Party. Wasn't irony grand?

"What's with the smug look? Are you listening to anything I have to say?" Maison's irritation was once again obvious.

Lang shook his head and then spoke in a manner which made it clear this conversation was coming to its conclusion. "William, you and your party are a paradox to me. But we do live in a democracy; you have many seats in Congress, so feel free to lay all your cards on the table with the American people, and if you do, I will be more than content to lay mine down."

The two sat staring at each other for a moment. It could have lasted an eternity had the intercom system had not activated. "Mr. President, Father Daniel Ananias is here for your one o'clock appointment."

Lang's eyes instantly brightened. "Thank you, Szandor. Please send him in."

Maison gazed at Lang with a sneer. "Oh, so you are taking orders from the Vatican, I see?"

Lang looked curiously back at the senator. "No, I am sorry to disappoint you, Senator. I would have thought your Catholic upbringing would have you better informed on the Church's understanding of her role in the political order."

He paused for a moment to watch for Maison's reaction, and the senator did not disappoint. Maison had never been reticent in expressing his disdain for a number of his own faith's teachings. Lang had wondered on more than one occasion why he did just not leave for some other form of Christianity.

"You know what I mean," Maison muttered through clenched teeth.

"Do I?" Lang was finding that he was enjoying this far too much. "Well, William, I must confess that I do relish the opportunity to ensure that my conscience is fine-tuned through many contacts with people of faith. But in this case, the truth be known, Father Daniel is a longtime friend of mine. My parents were missionaries in Iraq in my late teens. We had befriended a young Kurd back then, not long after which his parents were gassed by Saddam's regime. They helped get him out, eventually bringing him to America. And the rest, as they say, is history. Despite the plans of evil men, good came forth."

"Disgusting," Maison breathed, with a feigned sense of empathy. "What religion can drive a man to…"

"Disgusting," Lang countered, "what *power* can drive a man to…"

iii

Vanya walked apprehensively up the steps towards Jonathan's room. She peered in, finding him, as usual, sitting on his windowsill and staring off into nothingness.

"For Heaven's sake, Jonathan, it's been such a long time. You can't stay up here forever."

"Can't I?" he responded, turning towards Vanya. She could see tears in his eyes.

She moved towards him and sat on the bed. "Why don't you come with me to see Dr. Ilyushenko, if you could just—"

"I'm never going back to see him," Jonathan snapped. "He's screwed with me long enough."

Vanya was having a difficult time accepting this part of Jonathan. He had become so negative. This attitude had come and gone over the past seven or eight weeks, but something seemed to be eating away at him—something more than just Nathan's disappearance.

"This is not like you, Jonathan," she began, groping for words. "Is there something you aren't telling me?"

Jonathan had been looking down, but his interest seemed to be aroused by this last comment. He looked straight at his Aunt Vannie, staring in a manner which made her feel uncomfortable.

"Maybe there is something you aren't telling *me!*" He paused for a moment, then asked, curtly, "Who is my father?"

Vanya was caught off-guard for a moment, but then quickly responded. "I told you, he was a—"

"What you told me wasn't true. I can *feel* that it isn't true. What I want to know is who was, or *is*, my father?"

Vanya looked away, beginning to shake her head. "No, please don't ask about that anymore. I—"

"I *am* asking you. I have a right to know! You must tell me, *Mother*, is it... is Luther my... my *father*?"

Vanya felt herself begin to choke up. She continued shaking her head, blurting in intermittent bursts, "I... don't... know. I can't... be sure..."

"But you suspect it, don't you?" Jonathan was now up beside her, on the bed, grilling her persistently. "You believe that he is! Don't you?"

Vanya was almost on the verge of panic. "I... I..."

"Tell me!" he demanded. "Do you believe Luther is my father?"

Vanya, unable to get any more words out, clenched her teeth and slowly nodded.

Jonathan, eyes wide, lay back on his bed against the bedpost. Vanya got up and quickly exited the room sobbing.

She had reached the top of the stairs when Jonathan's cell phone rang. She steadied herself against the banister as she heard Jonathan's voice from his room.

"Hello?"

A moment of almost deafening silence followed. Vanya strained her ears to hear the next syllable escape from Jonathan's mouth.

"Nate!"

11

"There was a blind man who, merely by placing his hands upon an animal, could determine to what species it belonged. To test him one day, they brought him a wolf's whelp. Long and carefully he felt the beast all over. Then, still being in doubt, he said: 'I do not know whether thy father was a dog or a wolf, but this I do know, that I would not trust thee among a flock of sheep.'

— Aesop
The Blind man and the Whelp

i

"I do not understand how it is possible for him to say no to you, or to his calling."

Luther absorbed the words of one of his brother *Illumini*, Cato, attempting to understand himself what exactly was going on. Luther had grown uncharacteristically unsure of himself and did not relish the feeling at all. Even more importantly, he did not want the *Illumini* to be aware of his lack of insight into Jesse's soul.

"There is more going on here than we are aware of," Luther asserted. "I detect the hand of our Adversary in this impasse. Jesse is a part of me, and I can sense that in him. His shadowed side has grown strong, but some wall has been placed there which prevents this side of him, or should I say, his *true* nature from being brought forth."

Another member of the *Illumini*, called Marius, spoke up. "Do you believe that you can eradicate this wall you speak of?"

"Of that," Luther responded, "I have no doubt. But I am not going to take that measure, not just yet."

"And why not?" a third member, Anaxagoras, questioned.

"Because," Luther replied, slightly irritated at this grilling when the answers should have been obvious. "The wall is weakening even as we speak. If I am right, and our eternal Adversary is involved, Jesse's *own choice* to live out his true nature, his true destiny, will be much more valuable to us. He will have defeated the spark of light that is within him, and no one will be able to lift a finger to prevent the *Light-Bearer* from assuming full dominion over the Earth."

The one called Eumenes gazed intently at Luther. "And if he does not *choose* to fulfill his destiny with us?"

Luther looked off into the darkness and responded with a resounding note of intensity in his voice.

"Then I will stamp out what little spark remains myself!"

ii

"So when are you going to tell me where you've been staying?" Jonathan asked Nathan as the two drove down the familiar streets to the soup kitchen. Jonathan would not take the most direct route, as it was becoming more frequent to have stones thrown at the vehicle in certain sections of the town. His classic Mustang was still quite beaten up from the earlier accident, but a teenager having his own car was now quite rare—quite a luxury—quite a target.

"Why is that so important to you?" Nathan questioned with still a trace of suspicion in his voice.

Jonathan shrugged. "It's not, I guess. I'd just like to start writing and playing again. That's all."

Nathan eased up, responding to Jonathan in a more conciliatory tone. "I'm sorry, Jon-boy. I'm still a bit edgy. When my Aunt died, I-I just didn't want to be around anyone. You understand, don't you?"

"Sure, Nate," Jonathan spoke apologetically. "I didn't mean to pry."

"No problem, Jon-boy. And in response to your other comment, a friend of mine absolutely loved those demos we put together."

Jonathan looked over towards Nathan, unable to conceal his excitement. "You played it for someone and they liked it? Who? Is he into the music business? Is—"

"Slow down, ol' boy," Nathan interrupted with a laugh. "He asked if he could put down some keyboard tracks, and I told him, 'why the hell not?'"

"That's great! So we've got another member to our band! All we need now is a drummer!"

Nathan shook his head and smiled. "You're way ahead of the game, Jonathan. I never said he wanted to be *in* the band. In fact, I never said that you and me *were* a band. We—"

"We are, Nate," Jonathan asserted, almost dreamily, racing through thoughts and possibilities in his mind. Once again, his consciousness had drifted far away. "It's all coming together. I'd like to meet this guy, ahh..."

"Simon."

"Yes, Simon, of course. I'd like to meet him as soon as possible. Say, Wednesday?"

Nathan's expression was noncommittal. "I think he goes to his meetings Wednesday afternoon, but I suppose he'd be free after that. Not a lot of other exciting things going on in the life of a mechanic." Nathan thought a moment more, then shrugged. "Sure, why not. It might be fun just to jam a bit. But no promises!"

Jonathan smiled contently as he pulled up to the soup kitchen. He had Nathan right where he wanted him, and they both knew it. Nathan hopped out of the car.

"See you later tonight, okay?" Nathan stated as he began to exit to car.

"Sure, no—"

Jonathan's voice cut off. Nathan, realizing Jonathan had stopped in mid-sentence, turned back towards his friend. A perplexed look came to his face as he saw Jonathan's expression. His face had turned white, and he had his eyes fixed on something. Nathan began to move back towards the car.

"Jonathan? Is something...?"

But Jonathan could no longer hear Nathan. He was staring through the large front window of the soup kitchen. There, inside the dining area, amongst dozens of homeless souls, sat the old transient, the shabbily dressed man who had saved his life so many years before. He was bowed in prayer with another man, with both of his hands on the man's forehead. He mouthed inaudible words with his eyes closed.

Jonathan slowly stepped from the still-running car and headed for the entrance.

"Jonathan, what the hell's gotten into...?"

Again, he heard nothing. Jonathan was now inside the building, moving quickly and working his way through the throng of homeless people to get to the booth where he had seen the man. He finally broke through the crowd, arriving at the spot where he had seen the wretched-looking individual who had also been his mysterious savior.

Only he was not there. Jonathan quickly scanned the room, desperately looking for the familiar face, but it was nowhere to be found. Nathan broke through the crowd and caught a hold of Jonathan's arm.

"Jon! What the hell's going on? You just—"

"It was him!" Jonathan responded, still scanning the room. "It was him."

Nathan was perplexed. "It was who?"

Jonathan turned his gaze towards Nathan, still in a stupor. "The man who saved my life."

Jonathan caught sight of the person he had seen opposite his transient savior, and he quickly navigated through the crowd to catch up with him. He grabbed the homeless man's arm and spun him around.

"The man!" Jonathan gasped, excitedly. "The man you were praying with, where is he? Who is he?"

But the homeless man only smiled back. Jonathan searched his face for an answer and caught sight of a strange mark, some kind of tattoo, on his forehead. It was a capital 'P' with a lower case 'x' inscribed on the bottom half of it. For a moment, Jonathan felt himself captivated by the symbol.

"He can't tell you nothing."

Jonathan snapped out of the daze he was in, realizing that another homeless man was speaking to him.

"Wha?" he was able to manage.

"I said," the man continued. "He can't tell you nothing. His name's Jared. Poor bastard's deaf and dumb. Hasn't spoken a word since the day he was born. You know what deaf and dumb means, boy?"

Jonathan felt an embarrassing wave of self-consciousness sweep across him. "Y-Yeah, sure." He paused for a moment, and then addressed the man who had spoken to him. "Do you know the man who he... ahh... Jared was talking to?"

"Sure do. What's it worth to you, boy?"

Jonathan looked around and saw Nathan shaking his head no. However, he had no intention of allowing this opportunity to pass him up. He reached down into his pocket and pulled out a ten-dollar bill.

"What, you gonna give me enough money to buy a gumball?"

Jonathan provided an embarrassed nod and then digging again, pulled out a hundred-dollar bill.

"Wow!" the man responded, his eyes lighting up at the sight of the money. "You sure must want this guy bad!"

"His name?" Jonathan inquired sternly.

"Yeah sure. People call him 'Hanoch', some call him 'Mo'. Don't know his real name. Don't know if anyone does. He comes around here every now and then, praying with the folk here." The man paused, his eyes stealing a glimpse at Jonathan's torso. "You know, that sure is a nice coat you're wearing. I—"

But Jonathan was already moving away towards the exit. However, the instant he reached the doorway, a hand clasped his wrist.

"Aiyee!" Jonathan yelped, already having been spooked by the entire scene. He turned around to realize the homeless man, Jared, was clinging to his hand. Jared made a gesture with his free hand towards his left ear and leaned over towards the left side of Jonathan's face.

"Thank you," he whispered.

Jonathan was paralyzed in utter astonishment as he stared back at the homeless man's face. A moment later, the man called Jared let go and disappeared back into the crowd. Jonathan backed slowly through the entrance, still spellbound at what had just transpired. He bumped into a passerby, which quickly brought him to his senses.

"Watch where you're walking, asshole!"

Jonathan hesitated for a moment, and then quickly returned to his car. He briefly met eyes with a perplexed Nathan and took a deep breath before driving off.

iii

Samuel sat at the computer, at times typing relentlessly, then sitting back to hear his composition play. His room was a complete wreck; guitars, keyboard, drums, among other musical instruments and paraphernalia were strewn throughout the room.

"Samuel!" his mother yelled from downstairs. Her incessant nagging had become quite a bore to him. He turned the music speakers up several notches.

"I know you hear me, Samuel! I know you think I'm useless now that you've met your piece-of-shit father! But I am still your mother! You need to respect me, you arrogant son of a—"

Samuel cranked the music up several more notches, which made his windows vibrate. Yes, he had met his father, but no, he had not received his desired assignment, at least not yet.

"You must be patient, my son. Marvelous possibilities lie ahead for you…"

He didn't like being put off. In reality, no one other than Luther had ever responded to his offers to serve with anything other than blatant gratitude. It further exposed a point of weakness deep within him—a yearning that Samuel wished was never there. But he would wait. Patience was not a virtue he possessed in great abundance, but he was further towards his goal than he had been only six months prior. For now, he would continue to explore his own ventures and opportunities.

"You answer me, you little prick! I'm not one of your little whores who just—"

Samuel kicked up the sound system its final few notches.

"Yeah, *lo que tú digas* , Delilah," he breathed, then closed his eyes, letting the music encompass him.

12

Something touched me...
    I know not how
    I know not why
    But I remember when
    And I shall never be the same

Something moved me...
    When I feared I could be moved not
    When life had seemed
    A pre-written play
    In which I was destined to a tragic part

Something pierced me...
    From the inside out
    Discovering my pain
    Reflecting it back
    To eyes which refused to see

Something will not release me...
    For its purpose is not yet clear
    And my path not yet chosen

Though I
    In my arrogance
    Petition for Truth
    I hide
    Still
    Amongst the sleepy green meadows of fiction

DOMINION

i

"So then, I'm yelling at Jon, saying, 'What the hell are you doing?' and he looks back to me and says, 'I saw the man who saved my life!'"

Simon tried to restrain his laughter, but Nathan was such a good storyteller and master in his presentation of the absurd that he could not. Jonathan looked down, obviously embarrassed, yet smiling nonetheless.

"I'm telling you, Simon, Jon's a nice guy and all, but sometimes he gets just a bit psychotic."

"Well, then," Simon announced, holding up his bottle of tonic water, "here's to psychosis!"

Nathan smiled and held up his beer. Jonathan, feeling more at ease with Simon's good-natured comment, shook his head and followed suit, raising his beer to the others.

They all took a swig of their respective drinks and subsequently set them down.

Simon, somewhat excitedly, exclaimed, "You two wait here. I've got something for you." He hopped over the couch and scurried out of the room.

Jonathan looked to Nathan curiously, who simply shrugged his shoulders. Simon re-entered a moment later, holding a music disc in his hand. He popped it into his audio system, looked at Jonathan and Nathan enthusiastically, and plopped himself down on the couch.

What came out across the speakers was familiar, yet only slightly so.

Both Jonathan's and Nathan's respective expressions dropped into

84

looks of astonishment. Here, playing through Simon's system, were their voices, their instruments, but in a thicker and more melodic setting. An unobtrusive touch of synthesizer had been added, endowing the music with an almost classical flair.

"What the——?" Nathan began, but Jonathan quickly raised a finger to his lips, requesting—*demanding*—silence.

The piece (the term 'song' no longer sufficed) ended, and all three sat motionless, mesmerized by the sounds which had just touched their souls. Simon sat with a somewhat smug grin on his face and was the first to speak up.

"Jon, I know this bozo over here doesn't know didley about classical music, so I assume that you have some background in it."

Jonathan was having a difficult time absorbing any additional input. He could still hear the notes, melodies, and harmonies playing in his head. He cocked his head inquisitively. "I don't understand what you mean. *You* put the classical synthesizer in there... it sounded like orchestral instruments, I just——"

"No, Jon," Simon interrupted. "The piece you and Nathan composed already had a classical taste. It practically left me a roadmap for filling in the void."

"Damn," Nathan was finally able to get out of his previously dumbstruck mouth. "I'll admit—I didn't originally like the direction Jon was pushing my arpeggios. But that sounded awesome."

"So where do we go from here?" Jonathan asked. "You two are the music experts."

"Well," Nathan began. "This isn't exactly barroom music. It's too classy. It's probably closer to a mix between Old Alternative and New Age." He paused for a moment, contemplating. "I think we'd be better off completing a full demo disc and then circulating it."

"I'd have to agree," Simon added. "This is music you *listen* to, not just hear. It needs to be performed in a situation where the music is center stage— the main reason people come. A bar doesn't offer that kind of atmosphere."

"So what about percussion?" Jonathan questioned. "Do we just continue using the drum machine?"

Nathan sat back, thought for a moment, and shook his head. "No, I don't think so. Look what Simon's component added to the music. If we find the right drummer, maybe the music could take an even further leap."

Simon nodded. "A good percussionist could add power to the music, while also providing the light touch it needs at certain moments. A group called Pink Floyd came out with an album some years back and called it *The Delicate Sound of Thunder*. I think that's what we'd be looking for."

Jonathan lay comfortably on the couch, his hands folded behind his head. With a very content smile, he stated, "This feels so right. I know there's a lot to do, but for now, how about playing me the rest of the 'musical compositions' on that disc?"

ii

Annie D. tread slowly upon the ground leading to the final resting place of three loved ones. A light November dusting of snow was upon the Missouri soil. It reflected how her heart felt at the moment.

Her husband had purchased this land after the death of Yerik, desiring that their family be kept together—if not in life, then in eternal rest. After Yerik's funeral, the first thing Alexandre had done was bulldoze the house on the property to the ground—the house where all this suffering had begun. Now both dwellings in which their daughter and grandchildren had lived were no more. Whatever power her husband had to remove potential reminders of a terrible life, he would utilize and act upon swiftly.

Annie D. moved into the clearing, reaching the three plots up on the grassy knoll moments later. She stood at the foot of Tobias' grave with Marisha's on the left and Yerik's on the right.

"How are we doin' today, loves?"

The aching in her heart continued to grow. This was her first visit since the funeral four months prior.

"I find myself wishin' I was a wee bit more like me ma and da, God rest their souls. They saw many bad things in their family—aye, they did. But they did not enter into it."

A brief wind kicked up, which was uncharacteristically frigid for this time of year.

"Aye, they were persecuted. I s'pose we all were. But they would not pick up arms... they would not respond to hate with hate. So they kept me from it—*far* from it. So far that the rest of the family shunned us as well."

PHOENIX

The browning leaves on the many surrounding trees in the clearing began to rustle again, though this time Annie did not feel the wind. She looked at each stone; Marisha's looking fairly aged, Tobias' only a bit so, and Yerik's looking as fresh as a new day.

"My uncle, Yerik, you would have had a word or two to say to him. A hateful man. He didn't care a lick about who he hurt, so long as they were English; though I know there wasn't a shortage of Englishmen who felt the same way towards us. He gave my da hell, but me da didn't let it sour him."

Annie took a brief look back at the path to the old country road. She had told the driver she would not be long. She looked up to the sky to see the sun well below the tree line. Her body shivered as she shook her head.

"My da would be so disappointed in me. He thought he'd helped me avoid that life. But here I am! Violence! I never knew the man your da would become. He was just a hurt, frightened foot soldier." She wiped the moisture from her eyes, trying to keep her composure before her loved ones. "Yet now I've made me bed, and I have to sleep in it. I can't be pointin' fingers—I share the blame, especially for you, Yerik. You didn't want this life, either—I share the blame."

The interior pain had become overwhelming by this point, and Annie felt her knees buckle as she fell to the ground weeping. It was a good ten minutes before she thought she heard...

"Grammy."

"What? What was... who's talkin'?"

But there was nothing. Her eyes fell upon the headstone of Tobias. She felt a brief interior chill—a fright—but then her eyes wandered until they locked upon a tree just beyond the headstones. As soon as she fixed her gaze upon it, the momentary sense of fear was immediately overwhelmed with an intense maternal presence. A wave of consolation swept through Annie as the tree seemed to sway in the wind, despite the fact that there was no breeze at the moment. The rest of the trees surrounding the clearing stood motionless.

Annie D. stood from the place she had been kneeling, still fully taken by the tree she had somehow not noticed when she arrived. It was totally out of place. She moved to it, placed her hand upon its narrow trunk, and again felt a presence—a comforting, soul-piecing presence A sound not unlike wind chimes seemed to play a not-so-random, sad tune—though Annie was not sure if it was actually her ears or her heart that was hearing it.

"Your ways are mysterious, Lord," she whispered. "I can't say I'm too

pleased with You at the moment. You'll have some explainin' to do one day—
but I'll not leave Ya; really, where would I go?"

iii

Eliot Lige entered the office of Menachem Ashir, Prime Minister of
Israel, and his new superior. Lige had been nominated to his current post a little
more than two months before, and now that his position was confirmed, he was
anxious to get immersed in his new job as soon as possible.

"Good day, Mr. Lige. Please come in," Ashir greeted, motioning
towards a seat in front of his large desk.

"Thank you, Prime Minister."

Ashir responded very well to flattery and fully enjoyed the ranks and
privileges of his position. Lige was well aware of this fact, and used it to his
advantage.

"Have you been enjoying your new post?" Ashir questioned.

"Yes, sir, I have," Lige responded. "I would say up till now, for the
most part, I have just been familiarizing myself with the position."

"Well, I know you will do a good job. That is why I appointed you."

"You are too kind, sir."

Lige was aware of the fact that this explanation for appointing him was
not entirely true. In fact, his expected competence in the position had almost no
bearing on the decision. Lige was a Christian, but still of Jewish descent. With
the growing number of Christians in the Nation of Israel, coupled with Ashir's
declining popularity, the prime minister knew he needed the support.

Ashir continued. "As you know, these past seven years have been very
difficult for our nation. The Islamic expansion in the world threatens our very
existence in a manner not seen since the *Shoah*. They may have deceived the
leaders of Russia, Great Britain, Poland, and Portugal, even the Pontiff himself,
but I am not fooled. They have no intention in letting Israel continue its
existence."

"It would seem the expulsion of all Muslims from Israel was not taken
kindly by the followers of Mohammed."

Ashir looked at Lige intently. "We handed over all the disputed territories, save Jerusalem. Relocating—I think that is a much fairer term—the Muslims was the only thing that saved Israel from complete annihilation in the face of the Islamic Revolution. We had foresight! Great Britain did no less!"

"This is true, Prime Minister. And I pray that history—and the Good Lord—are kind to us for the decisions we have made."

Ashir nodded and proceeded, a bit more at ease. "Yes, I pray for the same." He leaned forward. "Listen, I am not going to mince words with you, Mr. Lige, as I begin to tell you what I must say."

"I appreciate your candor, Prime Minister."

Ashir nodded in acknowledgment. "More so than anything, I was elected to this office due to one pledge I made, and that pledge alone. I promised that I would be the leader responsible for the rebuilding of the Jewish Temple."

Lige nodded. "I do recall that promise."

"Yes, as does the rest of the Nation of Israel. Obviously, our Muslim 'friends' are less than keen on the idea. Of course, they expect us to allow them to rebuild the Dome of the Rock." Ashir leaned forward across his desk. "I cannot let that happen."

He held Lige's gaze for a moment before continuing. "I believe the Caliph—that butcher Ali Bakr—is quite aware of my intent. We have both remained somewhat quiet on the subject to the rest of the world. But behind closed doors..." Ashir paused, a bitter look beginning to surface on his face. "I would like to rip his heart out."

A mild look of surprise crept onto Lige's face. "Sir?"

"Yes, Mr. Lige, you heard me correctly. So few have the foresight—and the clear understanding of history—to read the signs of the times. Plainly speaking, I need the freedom to rebuild the Temple while still maintaining the peace."

Lige raised an eyebrow. "That is quite a tall order, Prime Minister."

"I understand that," Ashir agreed. "And to be honest, I do not care how far the peace is bent, so long as it is not broken. You do understand my position, do you not, Mr. Lige?"

Lige nodded. "I believe I—"

"Then I will put you in charge of the negotiations. Keeping me well advised, of course."

Lige looked at Ashir in a confused fashion. "Negotiations?"

"Yes, a young moderate, Ibn Fatimah, has been appointed Foreign Minister of the Islamic Union and has been empowered by the Caliph to act on his behalf. In a show of goodwill, our leaders in the Knesset are prepared to offer you the same authority."

Lige thought for a brief moment before speaking. "Sir, with a situation so potentially explosive and of such great magnitude, would it not be considered... inappropriate... for anyone besides yourself to head the talks?"

Ashir shook his head disinterestedly, "No, I do not believe so."

Lige sat for a moment. The situation was becoming clearer as he thought it through. He pondered for a moment on how to respond to Ashir, rapidly realizing that he was being led into a political trap.

Choosing his words carefully, he began to speak. "Sir, you have always been adamantly opposed to my involvement in 'Christians of Israel'."

Ashir nodded nonchalantly. "I oppose anyone who attempts to convert Jews from the True Faith."

Lige provided a subtle nod of acknowledgement. "I prefer to think of it as an invitation. Nonetheless, you still appointed me to this post without requiring that I resign my leadership of the organization."

Ashir again nodded, still in a disinterested fashion. Lige took a moment, realizing that he was about to tread on dangerous territory. He proceeded cautiously, though assuredly.

"If it is announced that I will head the talks with the Islamic Union, and these talks subsequently, and I might add *inevitably*, fail to achieve your desired results, then your greatest failure will be only that you appointed the wrong man for the job."

"I suppose it could be interpreted that way."

Lige continued, still maintaining an expression of serenity on his face. "I would be discredited as a leader, perhaps requested to resign my post—and maybe even be accused of not having the Jewish faith's best interest in mind. Would you say that is accurate, Prime Minister?"

"I do not know that I can truly speculate on the future, but I suppose that is a possibility."

"You, on the other hand, will be left relatively unscathed, and I am sure, apologetic for giving a Christian a chance in the Nation of Israel's government."

Ashir shook his head and smiled. "Mr. Lige, please, you are getting too far ahead of yourself, and in the wrong direction I might add. I have the utmost confidence in your ability to negotiate a deal which will give the Jewish faith back its Temple. My only question to you, my friend, is... is your heart Israeli?"

Lige paused, then stood, clasping his arms behind his back, and, looking momentarily skyward, responded in an official tone to the prime minister. "I have no question as to where my loyalties lie, Prime Minister, and I will serve in the capacity of this office to the best of my ability, so long as I have no questions as to where this office's loyalties lie."

Ashir, taken aback by this perceived insubordination, stood up slowly from his desk, moving his face closer to that of Lige's. "I think," he began in a stern tone, "that we both understand what the situation is, Mr. Lige. And I suggest that you keep your personal opinions on the political decisions of this office to yourself. I have informed you of your assignment. You are dismissed!"

13

"Turn your backs and keep your eyes shut tight;
for should the Gorgon come and you look at her,
never again would you return to the light."

– Dante
Inferno (IX-6,45)

i

"You know, Jon, *I* think it's great that you want to help out at the soup kitchen. But I've got to admit, I'm... umm... well, pretty skeptical about your motives. I haven't forgotten about your freak-out last time."

"Yeah, I know," Jonathan admitted in an amiable tone. "I don't know what got into me. Guess I've just been having a rough time recently. It won't happen again."

Nathan looked over at Jonathan with slight misgivings as they pulled up in front of the soup kitchen. "Okay, I'll go talk to my boss." He turned his head towards the back entrance. "Looks like he just got here. Remember, no promises!"

"None whatsoever."

Nathan hopped out of the car and jogged slowly into the building. Jonathan waited patiently, watching as the queue of homeless people began to form outside the front door.

A few minutes passed and Nathan was back outside the side door, beckoning to Jonathan. "He says okay, Jon, but he's got to go over a few things with you."

Jonathan smiled and swiftly located a parking space. He mimicked Nathan's slow jog, reaching the side door quickly.

"It's your lucky day, Jon, he's in a good mood," Nathan asserted with a mild tone of relief.

Nathan brought Jonathan into the back end of the kitchen, where giant vats were stewing the soup of the day. "Mr. Gabrielle?" He was addressing a large, balding man who wore a smock with enough soup spilled on it to feed a small family. "This is my friend, Jonathan."

Jonathan held out his hand, but Mr. Gabrielle did not shake it. "Pleased to meet you," Jonathan stated, drawing his hand back awkwardly.

"Yeah, whatever, kid," Gabrielle responded in a gruff voice. "Nathan here tells me you've had some run-ins with the law and have some community service to do."

Jonathan shot a quick glance at Nathan, who widened his eyes and gave a nod of encouragement.

"Well," Gabrielle continued. "I don't care much about that. Just get yourself a smock. You'll be serving the slop. Come back here and get another bucket when you run out, and any problems with the slummers, call the police. Got it?"

Jonathan looked at Gabrielle uncomfortably. "Ahh... yes, sir, not a problem."

Mr. Gabrielle turned around, resuming his task as Nathan pulled Jonathan towards the front. "Don't worry about him," he whispered.

"What was that all about?" Jonathan asked, a little annoyed with his friend.

"Listen," Nathan began. "Gabrielle doesn't believe that anyone does good for others unless there's something in it for themselves. He's on work release himself, and he'd be suspicious of you if you told him you just like to help others."

Jonathan still looked unsatisfied. Nathan recognized this and responded quickly. "Hey, Jon, you wanted in, I got you in. The customers are about to start coming in. You serve the soup, I'll do the drinks." Nathan provided a meek grin. "It'll be cool having you here."

Jonathan shook his head as he put on his smock. He took his first container of soup out, as Gabrielle had directed.

"Just let me know when you're getting low, I'll grab more!" Nathan yelled from the front door, where he began letting their homeless customers in.

Jonathan began serving, closely scrutinizing each individual he served, trying to pick out the man they referred to as 'Hanoch' or 'Mo'. After about ten minutes, and half his container of soup, a man slid in front of him with the same marking on his head as the other homeless person, Jared, had.

Jonathan stared at the symbol, feeling a sense of familiarity—as if he should recognize it from somewhere long ago, but he was unable to put his finger on its origin. The man broke his trance.

"May I have some soup please, sir?"

Jonathan blinked his eyes, trying to shake the brief feeling of vertigo. "I-I'm sorry. I was just... I was just wondering where you got that marking on your forehead."

The man smiled and responded. "Though I am but a poor soul, I have been granted the gift of life everlasting. I have prayed all my life that the Good Lord would allow me to lay eyes on you before the end of my days. I shall ask nothing more of my God." And with that, the man moved on.

Jonathan, bewildered by this statement, tried to follow the man with his eyes but quickly lost him in the crowd. He then realized that the next man in line had been speaking to... no... yelling at him.

"Hello! Earth to dumb-ass! Can I get some service here?"

Jonathan turned his head toward the man, and their eyes met. The man stopped speaking instantly, and the look of annoyance melted from his face. They continued to stare at each other while Jonathan mechanically reached the ladle into the small vat and provided the man with a bowlful of chicken rice soup.

A tear began to slide down the side of the man's face. "Thank you... thank you so much," he stated passionately as he moved on, quietly weeping.

The hours crept by, Jonathan feeling as if he were sliding in and out of some peculiar dream. Finally, a bellowing voice knocked him out of whatever state he was in.

"What the hell is going on here?" It was Gabrielle's voice. He came out of the back and up to Jonathan. "Kid! Are you serving these people or what? Todd tells me he's been waiting for you to come back and get more soup, and you haven't. It's been three hours, you should have been through eight buckets by now!"

Nathan, witnessing the commotion, stopped his activity and moved slowly over towards the pair. Gabrielle and Jonathan simultaneously looked down into the container with Jonathan's first batch of soup. It was still half full. They looked out across the soup kitchen and watched as the hundreds of homeless people sat, quietly consuming their soup.

Gabrielle looked back at Jonathan with an expression of astonishment. "What in God's name have you done?"

Jonathan looked back at him with equal astonishment. He had become aware that all the customers in the establishment were now silent, staring at him and Gabrielle.

"No," Gabrielle spoke, barely louder than a whisper as he backed away. "It's not in God's name at all, is it? It's the devil you serve!"

Jonathan, as perplexed as anyone, began to slowly shake his head, then looked over to see all of the homeless stand, then lower into a kneeling position before him. Gabrielle saw this and now possessed a look of terror as he began to reach under his smock. "Satan sent me a demon to slay!"

Before Jonathan realized what was happening, Gabrielle pulled out a small pistol from underneath his smock and fired at Jonathan three times.

Jonathan stumbled backwards from the blasts, then looked down to see three bullets lying in front of him.

"Get out of here, Jon!" Nathan screamed, running towards him.

He picked Jonathan up, and the two sprinted out the door and into Jonathan's car, still hearing Gabrielle's now hysterical voice screaming.

"A demon! He's a damned demon!"

ii

"It is, as the Americans say, *the damnedest thing*, Alex!" Felix Amosov ranted into his cell phone while driving along route 202.

"What are you babbling about, Felix?" Nesterov hollered back from the other end.

"He is here, Alex, that *sooka* is here!"

"Who?"

"Freeman!" Amosov replied jubilantly. "I just saw him!"

There was a pause on the other end of the line. Finally, Nesterov was able to respond. "How did you locate him?"

"That is what is so strange. He is here in Thyatira."

"What?" Nesterov asked in amazement. "He is living in Caputo's hometown?"

"Yes, would you believe it? I was just up here with a few of the boys, you know, visiting with his widow, paying my respects at the cemetery, and who drives by, but good old Harry himself!"

"This is incredible."

"It gets better! I hopped in my car and followed him home. I have his address—where he and his wife are living!"

"I cannot believe this! Can you really be sure, Felix? You know that they both had plastic surgery—"

"Yes, and it would appear that our source gave us accurate photographs of their new faces. A shame that the doctors did not make them look more Russian. But still, Alex, I had them quite committed to memory. These images are seared in my mind."

"This is just beyond belief!"

"Yet it is true! The Freemans are now living in the same town where our beloved boss is buried. Is that poetic justice or what? Anyway, I am ready to take out the both of them soon as you give the word."

Nesterov paused. "And what about the boy?"

"Boy? Oh yes, Freeman's son. No sight of him. He may be at school, or it is possible the Bureau may have split them up."

There was a pause from the other end of the phone. "I need all three taken out, Felix. I need to send a strong message back out to the other syndicates." Nesterov paused, thinking to himself. He shook his head and finished his thought out loud. "It has got to be all three, Felix."

"I understand, Alex. We will keep our eyes on them. If the kid does not come home, we should be able to *encourage* it out of old Harry—or at least out of his lovely wife."

iii

"Father! It's a scandal, so it is!"

Annie D. Nesterov was trying to remain respectful and calm, but she was not succeeding well at either. Having endured the death of a second child, her desire to restrain herself from expressing her opinions had all but waned. Life was too short to let nonsense by without so much as a word.

"Annie, I have no choice! We must do this to keep the parish open! You know the government took the nonprofit status away from all religious organizations. Nobody gives anymore because it is not tax deductible! And now we pay taxes on everything!"

Annie D. stared at the sign on the front lawn at the church.

OUR LADY OF SORROWS PARISH

Sunday Masses:	8:30 am	Sponsored by *MacroSoft*
	10:15 am	Sponsored by *Walbrowns*
	12:00 noon	Sponsored by *Flowers by Kings*

"Scandalous, Father!"

"Annie, please. I am not the one who makes the rules. The bishop has given us permission. In fact, he has even encouraged it."

"It's all a wee bit too weird to take in! I wonder what's next? A sneaker endorsement and logo on your chasuble? A banner coverin' the crucifix of our good Lord saying, 'Improve your love-life with *Vialis*!'?"

"Annie, please."

"I s'pose you'll be sayin' it's a sign of the times!"

The priest could only look down. "Perhaps, if your husband was to help us out a little—"

But he could feel Annie D.'s glare already.

"With all due respect, Father, you should be careful not to offer the devil an inch because God knows he'll trick you into givin' a mile!" Her tone changed to a more conciliatory one as she tried to suppress every part of her that was Irish. "I'll try to offer you just a wee bit of mercy for that comment. But you are sellin' out your Church with what you have done here. Don't make it worse by sellin' your soul. God will turn somethin' up. Live, hope, and don't worry."

14

i

Jesse was standing in his old home. The image from the darkest depths of his childhood was clearly still etched in his brain. He scanned the scene; he was standing in Tobias' room. Everything was exactly as he remembered it, only... smaller. Something *was* different, however. A warm breeze blew through the room, carrying with it an unpleasant stench.

Jesse began to move towards the window from where the wind seemed to enter the room. But as he moved closer, a sound stopped him. He turned his head to listen more closely.

Yes!

It was the unmistakable sound of a harpsichord playing.

With a touch of anticipation, Jesse scampered through the hall and down the steps. He slowed himself, peering around the corner as discreetly as he could. There, sitting on the piano stool with their backs turned to him, were his Aunt Vannie and...

"Tobias!" Jesse called out, unable to hold back.

Tobias barely responded, just looking up to their Aunt Vannie and smiling. Jesse took a step closer then suddenly froze. He found that he could no longer move his feet. Bewildered, he called out.

"Aunt Vannie! Help me!"

Vanya's head slowly shook from left to right. Jesse was about to call out again when a painful movement in his belly prevented him from doing so. The movement was much more intense than any intestinal discomfort he had felt before. Jesse looked down in horror to see his abdomen moving in strange and rapid contortions.

He looked up, no longer able to speak, as the first rip in his stomach sent a spurt of blood onto the floor. As the tear grew, Jesse heard the sound of violent growling escape from inside his abdomen. Suddenly, the seam ripped fully open and out from the gaping hole in his belly sprang a full-grown jackal. The jackal leapt from the floor upon an unsuspecting Vanya and Tobias.

The jackal viciously ripped into their flesh as each began to scream in agonized terror. Jesse again attempted to scream out, but he could not. His feet and hands were still immobilized. He watched helplessly as his aunt and brother shrieked frantically. Then, as the limbs were torn from their bodies, something changed. They were no longer screaming in terror. They were... they were...

Laughing.

Not just laughing, laughing *hysterically.*

"NO!" Jesse was able to finally get out, but it was too late. He continued to struggle to move, but he still could not. Eventually he looked down to his feet and realized he was now elevated off the ground. His feet were pinned, one on top of each other, by a large nail.

Jesse gawked in dismay at his outstretched hands, screaming out as he came to the realization that he was nailed to a cross.

PHOENIX

The jackal, with bits of flesh and blood still dripping from its mouth, turned. In a leisurely fashion, it crept towards Jesse, now sobbing and writhing in pain. The jackal opened its mouth, from which a hauntingly familiar voice came forth.

"Do not deceive yourself, Jesse. You are responsible…"

ii

Nathan attacked the drums relentlessly, sometimes hitting, sometimes missing. Simon stood in the kitchen, finishing up the last of the dishes, wincing as he listened to his friend banging away. They had finished off the last of the Thanksgiving leftovers from his small celebration at his Uncle Garf's. Despite President Lang's reinstatement of the holiday, it had seemed that he and his uncle were the only ones continuing the tradition.

Simon ambled into the next room with his hands over his ears. Nathan looked up briefly, sweat dripping from his brow. He made a valiant, yet vain effort to end with a brilliant finale. Instead, his cymbals tumbled onto the ground with a crash. Nathan gracefully followed this feat by knocking over his snare drum in an attempt to save the cymbals. The room finally grew silent as he sat there, at the peak of frustration with sticks in hand, looking over to Simon.

"If it's all the same to you, I think we'll just add a light drum-line to our music with a drum machine," Simon contended, trying to get a smile out of Nathan.

Nathan did not smile back but looked at Simon with an expression of aggravation. "I'm ready to forget the whole damn thing!"

Simon, ever the serene one, paused before he replied. "Whatever's up with you, man, you've got to get it out. Don't keep torturing yourself—and me—for it."

Nathan looked down and released an exasperated sigh. Simon, though sometimes appearing the space cadet, was usually pretty astute when it came to reading people. "It's Jon. I don't know what's gotten into him. He's been pulling some strange crap—he says he wants to get a band together, but I haven't heard from him in two weeks." Disheartened, he looked back to Simon, "I thought I knew the guy, but now I wonder."

Simon shrugged. "Maybe he's having a hard time. Maybe he's—"

"Maybe we need to get someone else!"

Simon looked at Nathan and shook his head. "Dude, you know better than that. Jon's the one that has the ability to link the music you play with mine—at least in a way that doesn't sound like chaos."

But Nathan just shook his head. "I just think he doesn't know crap about the commitment you need to make in order to be in a band."

"Is this just about the band?"

Nathan looked up curiously and was about to respond when a rock crashed through the window. Already on edge, Nathan reacted immediately, sprinting through the front door.

"Nate! Hold on!"

But Simon's words fell on deaf ears. Nathan sprinted after two teenagers running from the house. With a diving tackle, he was able to pull the slower of the two down.

"You like breaking windows, kid?" he screamed as he pulled the youngster from the ground. "Well I like breaking faces!"

He swung at the youth, connecting squarely with his jaw. The youth fell to the ground and attempted to scramble away when Nathan stepped forward and kicked him in the ribs. Nathan was unaware of Simon screaming from his porch.

The youth lay still on the ground, panting. Nathan, still filled with rage, grabbed the kid by his long black hair. He cocked his arm, preparing to give this juvenile delinquent one last blow to turn his lights out. However, something prevented him from doing so. Someone had grabbed his arm.

"Stop it, Nate! What are you doing?"

Nathan turned, dropping the boy, and saw Jonathan standing before him. He barely missed a beat. "Well look who it is! What do you care, you damned quitter?"

Jonathan displayed a contrite expression on his face. "Listen, I'm sure you're ticked, but hey, let's just chill-out a bit. You know, go inside and talk..." Jonathan hesitated, looking at the youth still lying on the ground. "What's this all about?"

Nathan wiped the fresh dirt from his face. "Asshole threw a rock through Simon's window for no damned reason. A whole pack of these hoodlums do this stuff all the time. Someone's got to send them back a message."

Jonathan looked down again at the boy. "What's your name, kid?"

The boy sat up. Blood was streaming from his nose and down onto his black 'Judas Priest' shirt. "What's it to you?" the boy responded, though after seeing the expression on Nathan's face, he thought better of his attitude. "Joey," he responded in a raspy voice. "Joey Escario."

"Well, Joey-Joey Escario. Why don't you come in and get yourself cleaned up?" Jonathan glanced at Nathan for a moment. "I guess we're going to have to call your parents."

"Good luck finding them," Joey responded, picking himself up.

Nathan jumped in angrily. "Parents? I'm calling the damned police!"

Simon had just walked up behind the group. "Man, it's no big deal, these things happen. I'm not real—"

"Hold on a second, guys," Jonathan interrupted. "Joey, what do you mean 'good luck' calling your parents?"

"I mean just that, good luck! I don't know where the hell they are. I live in a shitty foster home."

"Keep talking like that and you're not going to be living at all!" Nathan retorted.

The youth smirked at Nathan defiantly. "Bite me."

Jonathan and Simon grabbed Nathan as he attempted to lunge at the boy. Joey just smiled at him.

"Get a hold of yourself, Nate! He's just a kid!" Jonathan yelped.

Nathan stopped struggling, then shook free of the two. He gave a disdainful look to Joey, and then turned back towards the house. Jonathan put a firm hand on the Joey's shoulder. "Let's go inside."

Nathan and Jonathan spoke to each other in the kitchen while Simon cleaned Joey up.

"You're never calling, you're not coming to practice! This was your idea, Jon!" Nathan stated in a less-than-pleasant tone.

Jonathan nodded his head. "I know, Nate, I've been having some... some problems."

"We all got problems, man, but if you really believe in the music, you've got to put them aside. It's not just talent that makes people successful in this business. It's *tenacity*!"

Jonathan stood, contemplating this thought. He looked off to his left, his mind seemingly light years away. The dream had not let go of him. After what seemed like an eternity, he spoke.

"You know, Nate, when I look back through my childhood, I realize that often the only peace I found was from the music. I don't know what it is about the notes, the melodies, the rhythms... they just seemed to cut through all the garbage I was feeling and slip straight through to my soul. It was like the music knew my pain, reflected it back to me, and then healed it within me."

He paused, chuckling lightly to himself before looking back to Nathan, who was listening intently.

"I've got to do this, Nate. It's a part of who I am. I feel something is inside of me that needs to get out, and the music is the vehicle for that to happen."

Nathan released the last bit of frustration from his spirit, allowing a hint of a smile to slip across his face. He began to nod his head. "You're right, Jon. I'm sorry about all this crap; it's just that I want this as bad as you do. I just want to make sure you aren't going to take off when something more interesting comes along."

"I understand... really... I do."

The two stood there for a moment without speaking. It was Nathan who broke the dual reverie.

"So where do we go from here?"

"Well," Jonathan began. "In all honesty, I'll probably need another week or two to get my own 'house in order', so to speak, then I'll belong to the band—heart and mind."

Nathan provided his signature sly smirk. "What about soul?"

Their conversation was interrupted by a booming sound from the next room. Someone was playing the drums.

He's not just playing them, Jonathan thought to himself. *He's experiencing them.*

Jonathan and Nathan moved into the next room, where they found Simon sitting on his couch, looking up in awe at the drum set. Sitting on the drum stool, going at it on the drums, was little Joey Escario.

But it was not just hard banging noises that were emerging from the drums, but a soft touch which carried its own form of quiet power with it. The steady, penetrating beat of the bass drum coupled with a light roll of the cymbals created its own dichotomous mood of power and tranquility. An occasional offbeat at times on the tom-toms produced a touch of discord which, instead of moving towards chaos, seemed to foreshadow transition.

Simon looked up at the other two with a grin extending from ear to ear as Jonathan eased onto the couch. Joey finished off with a dazzling—yet still fully controlled—crescendo, and then there was silence.

Jonathan paused for a moment with a somewhat spaced-out look on his face. "Nate?"

"Yeah?" Nathan responded, still mesmerized himself.

"Why don't you call Joey's foster parents and tell them that we may be bringing him back a little late."

Joey looked at each of the three's faces with an insecure curiosity. Sensing their approbation, he broke into a large, slightly embarrassed grin.

15

Enter Ye...

Into my realm

Of sin

Shame

Desires...

    Not asked for

    But given

    As my cross to bear

Innocence...

    So precious

    So rare

    So attractive

    So wrong

        My Wrong

        My Burden

Hope...

    A release

        From overwhelming pain

    An opportunity

        To understand

        To feel

        To grow

        To overcome

I accept my challenge

And pray for the strength

    To endure

        My Personal Demon

PHOENIX

For what is Faith?
.....if never doubt
What is hope?
.....if never failure
What is love?
.....if never loss

God.
Be with me in my Struggle
As I am striving
Ever onward
Growing closer
To You.

— Jonathan Corban Storm
Cross

i

Jonathan sat in his bedroom, looking out past the endless sea of stars. Thousands of questions streamed through his consciousness. He needed answers. Tonight he would journey.

He got up and stood at the window, still hesitant. Torn between his yearning to know and his desire to fade back into the safety of ignorance, he allowed himself to drift.

It was a curious mystery. Since he was young, Jonathan had had the ability to wander to another place, that plane of existence where his mother and Tobias waited for him. This had been the only door which he had stepped through. But following his horrible dream two weeks ago, he had sensed this door closing itself to him.

However, another portal now existed within him. Jonathan had exited through it months ago, never understanding how he had reached that murky place to begin with. This was the door to Luther. It remained open, just a crack, and morbid thoughts from that other existence had slowly been seeping through into his consciousness.

He felt a warm rush of air as the stars before him twinkled, slowly slipping out of focus. He steadied himself, overcoming a brief sense of vertigo as the flickering images of light around him came back into focus. He was now standing among thousands of candles.

Jesse heard the delicate sound of wind chimes playing a soft, not quite unfamiliar, melody. He looked up at a throne, where Luther sat before him.

"My son!" Luther began, unable to conceal his excitement. *"You have come to me!"*

Jesse responded, attempting an air of serenity. *"Only to seek answers. Nothing more."*

Luther's eyes narrowed momentarily, but he could not restrain a devilish grin from creeping across his face. *"I see."* He examined Jesse's face, reading his thoughts. *"You no longer resist the fact that I am your father..."*

Jesse looked up to him, fighting back the tears beginning to well up on his eyelids. He could not afford to show weakness. *"No,"* he whispered.

Luther smiled in an acquiescent fashion. *"I understand that this must have been a difficult step to take, Jesse, but you will soon find that there has been a great deal on which you have been... misinformed."*

Jesse wrapped his arms around himself and nodded slowly as the first tear dripped from his left tear duct. *"Every cell of my being tells me you are evil, Father."*

Luther closed his eyes and inhaled, gently savoring the sound of the word 'father' coming from Jesse's lips. *"No Jesse, not evil... opposing."*

Jesse looked curiously at Luther as he continued to speak.

"And I would venture to guess that it is not every cell of your being that pushes you into this line of thinking. I stand opposed to the current worldview which has been dominant in our existence for more than two millennia." He paused. *"Perhaps it is best understood through an ancient Chinese concept known as the Yin and the Yang."* Luther arose from his throne and began to wander amongst the candles.

"The Yin and the Yang, my son, are each alternate, opposing forces, but neither is good nor bad in and of itself. The Yin possesses a touch of Yang, and vice versa. You, Jesse, are that 'touch' which has been surrounded by the opposing force. This has made your life very confusing, but..." Luther paused long enough to meet Jesse's gaze, *"you will also find that it has made you stronger!"*

Their eyes locked, and something unspoken was exchanged between the two. *"I am here to bring you back to the fold."*

Jesse absorbed this information. It *did* somehow make sense to him. So much so that it unsettled him greatly. Yet at the same time, was he feeling a slight sense of… *affirmation?*

"I know this must be confusing to you. Being raised amongst the alternate force will do that. But you never were a part of that, Jesse. It was not who you are. You have always experienced this world as an outsider."

Jesse slowly nodded. This was true. He was not like the others.

Luther continued to saunter through the candles, circling behind Jesse. *"It felt good to give that deaf-mute his hearing and voice back, did it not? And feeding all those hungry people... I am telling you, my son, it is only the beginning."*

The scene moved, with the more and more familiar sense of brief vertigo returning, and suddenly they were again atop the high plateau, looking down upon the nations of the Earth. *"Join me, my son, and all that you see before you is yours to rule. For it is mine to give."*

Jesse looked about him, feeling the icy fingers of power and desire gently, no, *obstinately*, tug at his soul. Was this his destiny? This was an opportunity to rule over all that he knew. To set things straight in the world. *God knows, the world could use some order,* Jesse thought to himself.

His lips trembled as his impulse to accept Luther's offer slithered upwards from his vocal chords. But at the last instant, something quite different escaped from his tongue.

"And where does the man Hanoch fit into this whole thing?"

Luther's face contorted. *"Who? What are you talking about?"*

Jesse felt the icy fingers loosen their grip.

He doesn't know!

"I-I'm sorry, Father. I need more time to think."

A scowl slid across Luther's face. *"You still let them chain you, my son."*

Jesse recognized the slightest twinge of desperation in Luther's voice. He stepped back, focusing himself for his return. *"I've got to go. I've got to—"*

Jesse felt himself being drawn back forcefully from the scene, *feeling* the voice of his father one last time.

"Remember, my son. You came to me..."

ii

Violet Freeman awoke to the sound of a dog barking. She blinked her eyes several times, then looked towards the digital alarm clock on the night table. It read 1:19 a.m.

She would usually be somewhat annoyed at having been awakened, but this time she had been trapped in the middle of an unpleasant dream. Nathan had been in trouble, crying out for help, but she found herself unable to reach him.

She rolled out of bed and carefully moved towards the window overlooking the neighbor's house, where the dog continued to bark. At first glance, she saw very little. Then, as she looked up the street, she saw two unfamiliar cars parked on the near side of the road.

A wave of fear passed through her. Violet ran towards the front window, and sure enough there was another car parked in the opposite direction with two men standing outside of it.

"Oh, my God!" she shrieked, trying to squelch her own voice.

Harold sat up with a start. "What? Huh?"

He blinked his eyes, trying to shake the last bit of sleep from them. He too, had experienced unsettling dreams. He looked in his wife's direction, who was now scurrying back towards him with an expression of terror on her face.

"What's wrong, honey?" he asked anxiously.

"They're here!" she responded in a petrified whisper. "They've found us!"

A terrified look of realization came across Harold's face as he jumped towards the window. As he peered out, for just an instant he saw a figure duck behind the bushes near his front door. Harold ducked himself and turned back towards his wife.

"Quick!" he whispered harshly. "Call the emergency number!"

Violet nodded in acknowledgment, and, grabbing the phone, clumsily punched out the numbers. As Harold crawled towards her, a look of quiet desperation came across her face as she hung the phone up.

"It's dead," she stated, her mind starting to swirl.

"The cell phones!"

PHOENIX

"They're—dear God, they're in the car!"

Harold froze. This was it. The many years of running and fear were now coming to an end. He moved up towards his wife, who now appeared to be slipping into a state of shock, and leaned against the bed, not taking his eyes off of her.

Harold had only momentarily broken his stare from Violet, now looking listlessly down at the floor, when a terrifying thought hit him like an eighteen-wheeler.

Nathan!

"Oh my God!" he yelped in a voice which knocked Violet out of whatever world she had drifted into.

She stared at him, and a desperate look of realization came across her face. "Nathan!"

Harold thought for a terrifying instant, then jumped up towards the closet. "Quick!" he instructed while fumbling through the top shelf. "Get all the pictures we have of Nathan—any pictures from Pergamum. I'll be back in a minute."

Harold pulled a pistol from the closet and opened the bedroom door a crack. Before Violet could get out the second syllable of his name, he had slipped out.

She quickly moved towards the safe, where all their family albums and personal materials were kept, taking a moment to thank God that they had decided to keep all this identifying information in the bedroom. She opened the safe and then began ripping out photos and documents, shredding them to pieces.

She grabbed a metal trashcan from the bathroom and was fumbling for a lighter in her purse when she heard a gunshot ring out from downstairs.

"HAROLD!" she screamed out instinctively.

She sat, frozen, as she heard footsteps sprinting up the stairs. The bedroom door opened, and without thinking she lunged at the figure as it came in the door. A gunshot went off as they both fell to the floor. Violet began scratching violently at the figure's face when she recognized Harold's voice.

"Violet! There's not much time. Where's the lighter?" he shrieked.

She stared at him for an instant and was struck by the smell of gasoline. She looked down and saw a half-filled gas can on the floor, spilling out, which

Harold had brought up.

Violet scrambled back towards the pictures, and she heard the front door crash as intruders kicked it in. Harold began quickly dousing the entire room in gasoline. She promptly returned to him with the lighter. Harold shook the can, getting a sense of how much gasoline was left, then moved towards the bed.

Automatic weapons fire suddenly tore through the windows as he ripped a piece of cloth from the sheets. The gunfire stopped as quickly as it had started. Harold picked himself up off the floor, after having dropped instinctively. He could no longer see his wife.

"Violet!" he screamed.

Violet Freeman was able to pick herself up to her knees, but then she slumped down again. She had taken at least three rounds in the back. Harold crawled briskly across the floor to his wife. He could hear footsteps all over the downstairs, as well as a good deal of yelling.

"Violet?" Harold cried desperately. She turned her head slowly and smiled at him. "It's finally over," she whispered.

Harold looked at her with an expression of despair. "I can't—" he began to blurt out.

"Nathan," she whispered.

Harold looked up as he heard footsteps coming up the stairs. He froze for just an instant, then scrambled across the floor for his pistol. He heard a few cries as he fired every bullet remaining in his weapon through the bedroom door.

Pulling a bottle from his robe pocket, Harold filled it with the gas remaining in the can. He quickly doused the cloth he had torn from his sheets in gasoline, sticking it in the opening of the bottle. He moved quickly across the room to where his wife lay, now looking dreamily up at him. He choked back an urge to sob as he pulled the lighter from her hand.

He ignited the end of the cloth. The room lit up with the brightness of the flame. He stood and scooted towards the bedroom door. He hesitated for a moment, then yanked the door open and pitched his Molotov cocktail out into the corridor.

There was an instant flash of light as the ignited bottle smashed across the already gasoline-doused hallway. Harold heard screams and rapid gunfire as he crawled back towards his wife.

PHOENIX

Flames snuck under the door and began spreading throughout the room. He dragged Violet into the far corner.

"Is Nathaniel safe?" she whispered, barely audible.

"Yes, Honey, Nathan's going to be okay," he responded as the tears began to flow.

Harold pulled another box of cartridges out of his robe pocket and placed two in the clip of his pistol. He tossed the remaining cartridges across the room. Sobbing, watching how beautifully the light from the flames flickered across Violet's face, he popped the clip into the pistol.

Harold slowly raised the pistol up to the temple of his wife of twenty years, now weeping evenly. A look of understanding came across Violet's face as she closed her eyes.

"I love you," she whispered.

"As I do you, my love..."

16

i

"So he came to you of his own free will this time?"

"Yes," Luther responded, obviously pleased by the recent turn of events.

He stood before the *Illumini* once again, but this time with a greater sense of his place among them. His spiritual growth was proceeding well, perhaps nearing the point where he no longer would need the approval of this council.

The room was completely darkened, except for a half-dozen candles and the incandescent light which radiated from the *Illumini*.

"He is on the verge of acceptance of his true destiny," Luther added.

"There is very little time for delay at this point, Luther."

"I understand that, Brother Eumenes. I require two more cycles to fulfill what has been asked of me by our Master. If he refuses to bow down before me at that time, of his own free will, I will take what is rightfully mine."

The *Illumini* paused for a moment, seemingly in deep contemplation. They simultaneously rose from their seats, encircling Luther.

The *Illumini* called Cato then spoke. "You, Grand Elder Luther, final member of our coterie, are the cornerstone of the Brotherhood. It is through you that the Great Seraph speaks. You have deferred to our wisdom to this point. But on the day which your son becomes one with us, it is we who will defer to you, the voice, the Great Prophet of the Ancient One!"

PHOENIX

At this moment, each member of the *Illumini* dropped to one knee before Luther.

"We await the deliverance of the Anointed."

ii

Jonathan quivered in a fetal position in the far corner of his room. As much as he had tried, he could not re-open the door in his mind which had led to his mother and brother. What made matters worse was that now the portal that linked him with his father had grown much larger.

His night was filled with terrifying dreams. His day was saturated with morbid thoughts, constantly flowing in and out of his consciousness. The conflicting concepts became too much for him, and he finally withdrew into himself, no longer sure of which stimuli were real, and which came out of the darkest depths of his tortured soul.

"He's been this way since I woke up this morning, Viktor."

"Feel my presence, my son, feel your true destiny in me."

"It appears he has had a psychotic break."

"Brother!"

"What can be done for him?"

"Don't kid yourself, Jesse. You are responsible..."

"I can medicate him, for now."

"You're in for it now, you little son-of-a-bitch!"

"Has anything like this ever happened to him before?"

"You are my SON!"

"No... well, not since he was younger."

"Why, Jesse? Why did you let me die?"

"Following the abuse?"

"Jon's a nice guy and all, but sometimes he gets just a bit psychotic."

"I-I don't know, I guess it must have been. What's that you're giving him?"

115

DOMINION

"AAAAAAAAAAAAAAAAAAHHHHHHHHHHHHHHHHHH!"

Jonathan's thoughts were swept into a whirlpool as sirens went off in his head. For an instant, there was a tremendous sucking sound, and then all the noises immediately dispersed. His eyes focused on two figures standing before him. They both leaned in towards him with disfigured, demonic-looking faces. Jonathan tried to scream out in terror, but the image blurred and quickly faded as his entire consciousness collapsed in upon itself.

"What happened?" Vanya asked in a panic.

"I gave him a type of sedative. It should help him rest," Dr. Ilyushenko responded. "You said these episodes have happened before?"

"Yes," Vanya answered, obviously distraught. "When he was much younger."

"How did he come out of them before?"

"Well, I just wouldn't leave his side. Neither I nor Tobias did. And well I, I also..."

Ilyushenko looked at Vanya, curious as to why she had stopped. "Go on."

"I don't suppose it had much to do with it, but I would always play the harpsichord for him. He loved that harpsichord. I would just sit him down and keep playing. I'm sure it didn't have anything to do with it. It was probably more for myself."

Ilyushenko raised an eyebrow. "No, no, it may very well have helped. Therapists have been using music as a tool for a long time. It seems to have a way of reaching parts of us which are unreachable by other means." Ilyushenko paused. "Do you still have the harpsichord here?"

"No," Vanya responded sadly. "I'm sure it burned with the rest of the house."

"Well, Vanya, I can medicate him and do my best to work with him, but I am a full believer in going with whatever intervention has worked in the past. Do you follow me?"

"Yes," Vanya responded solemnly.

Ilyushenko paused and then looked back towards Jonathan. "I will come back to check on him tomorrow. For now, please, help me get him back into his bed."

iii

Nathan, Simon, and Joey sat in a small circle, listening to the last few notes of their song, which played out across Simon's audio system. Joey's percussion had been the final touch. They smiled at each other, and Simon stood to flip the switch off.

"That sounded awesome!" Joey stated, reaching over to grab Nathan's beer off the coffee table.

Nathan smacked his hand away. "Easy there, little man."

Simon nodded. "Yeah, it does sound pretty cool… even way cool. I see a future in it."

Nathan looked at Simon with a contemplative expression. "Yeah, but something still isn't quite right. I can't quite figure it out. It's like we got the right chemicals but not yet the right chemistry."

"Why the hell you gotta bring school into this?" Joey remarked, a light smirk on his face.

Nathan rolled his eyes.

"I heard," Simon began, "that Pax Romana once went on tour *before* they released an album, trying out their song compositions on stage, working out the kinks, getting into sync, until their songs evolved into what they put on the album."

Nathan mulled this point over for a bit. "Yeah, but as we're not established, like Pax Romana was, I can't see any ongoing playing forum which we can use. Like we said before, this isn't exactly barroom music."

"Not by a long shot," Joey jumped in as he lay back on the couch flipping through his *Classic Metal* magazine. Though there still seemed to be some residual feelings of animosity between him and Nathan, Joey, feeling affirmed for the first time in his life, was little by little allowing the more ingratiating dimensions of his personality to emerge. He had quickly become the mascot of the crew.

"Who said we have to play in front of anybody?" Simon queried. "We just have to play together more."

Joey put his magazine down and looked at Nathan. "So what about this Jonathan guy? You know, the guy who saved my life? Is he with us or not?"

Nathan did not immediately respond. "I spoke to his mom this morning. He's sick. *Real* sick. But if we're going to do this, we're going to do it with Jon, or we don't do it at all."

Simon nodded. "I agree. Jon's our hub."

Joey shrugged. "Well, you know he's *my* hero… well, him and J.J. Hambon. So what do we do for now?"

Nathan looked up at Joey as a smirk began to develop across his face. "Play music, you dumb-ass."

17

Free Euro Press ~

PATMOS - The United League of Democratic Nations became a reality yesterday as the leaders of the ten-nation confederacy signed the much-anticipated charter amidst unprecedented security.

The United States of America was the last to join the other nine nations: Great Britain, Ireland, Poland, Uganda, Portugal, Russia, the Philippines, Honduras, and Australia. This charter was seen by many as the first formal act signifying the United States' emergence from its isolationist policies. Many have attributed the free expansion of radical Islam as well as the resurgence of Communist Socialism throughout most of the world to these U.S. policies.

"Today's covenant between our nations is a statement on the dignity of each human life and the right to self-determination, both as individuals and nations," President Hugh Jennings Lang stated in a brief press conference following the signing. "Though we are always open to dialogue with those who believe differently, we today reject all forms of totalitarianism—be they overt or covert—which strip man of this inherent dignity, endowed by our Creator."

The confederacy has not been without its detractors, the most outspoken of whom is U.S. Senator William Maison. "While we acknowledge the necessity of mutual understanding among peoples, we vehemently reject the dangerous and inflammatory air of superiority that this charter reflects, as well as the divisive references citing a deity being the source of human rights."

DOMINION

i

Vanya opened the box containing the synthesizer that she had purchased as Jonathan lay comatose in his bed. She had not played a single note since Tobias had died. On that day, many of the usual pleasures in her life had vanished. But things were different now, and once again she would turn to the same source of consolation she had used more than a decade before to draw Jesse out from the terrifying darkness which encompassed him.

She placed the synthesizer on the desk situated near Jonathan's bed, flipped the switch, and after a brief search, pressed the button that coincided with the harpsichord sound. Vanya was not surprised, yet still somewhat disappointed when the sound which came out of the instrument did not fully reflect the richness of an actual harpsichord. Still, she began to play, shaking the old cobwebs from her mind and fingers.

The first few hours she played, she did not recognize any visible changes in Jonathan. He continued to lay motionless, an I.V. serving as his only nourishment, compliments of Dr. Ilyushenko. Yet she persisted on, slowly recalling the intricacies of the different pieces she had neglected for so long.

As she persevered with playing into the late afternoon, Vanya glanced over towards Jonathan and noticed something different. She abruptly stopped, getting up to walk over to the bed. His body had not moved, but there was now an expression on his face—a troubled expression.

As she looked down upon him, the expression slowly faded until Jonathan resumed his expressionless catatonic state. Her eyes widened, and she scurried back to her synthesizer, resuming her performance for her audience of one.

Her tired hands now had new life breathed into them, and Vanya hammered away at the keys, gratefully reveling in her newfound hope.

ii

"*Ebanatyi pidaraz!* I wanted them alive! I cannot get information from a dead person!"

Alexandre Nesterov was livid beyond any degree his men could recall. He had assembled his significantly reduced posse to find out how they had managed to botch the Freeman operation. The condition of his grandson was still at the forefront of his mind, which did not do much to help his already ruffled disposition.

"So what the hell happened?" Nesterov bellowed, staring directly at Felix Amosov.

"Well, Mr. Nesterov," Amosov began (he always referred to his boss by his proper name in front of the other men). "One of our boys got a bit excited and unloaded his z-sly through the bedroom window. It basically went downhill from there, but I am certain Freeman set the house on fire himself. He must have turned the gas stove on downstairs. We saw the house catch fire, and within a minute, the whole place exploded."

Nesterov slumped down in his chair and buried his face in his hands, more out of frustration than any sentiments of sadness. "How many did we lose?"

Amosov glanced at the other half-dozen men in the room. "Five in all. We lost Loutchnasky, Yegorov, Tambov, Likhodev, and Tenorio."

Nesterov shook his head, not saying anything. He knew his only chance of re-establishing himself among the battling syndicates would be through precise, clean, and effective operations. Losing five of his own men while eliminating only two of his three targets did not appear too impressive.

As if reading his boss' thoughts, Amosov responded, "We removed the bodies of our boys—no one needs to know what has happened. Also, we retrieved this."

Nesterov looked up as Amosov placed a wallet-sized picture on his desk. Nesterov reached over to pick it up, slowly looking over the picture of a longhaired teenager.

"This is Freeman's son?" he asked, not taking his gaze from the picture.

"Yes, sir," Amosov responded, finally feeling confident enough to slip a piece of his nicotine gum into his mouth. "We retrieved it from a local dry-cleaners. Apparently Freeman had left his wallet in his suit jacket pocket when he turned it in that evening for cleaning. We intercepted the call to his mobile phone—which he evidently left in his car—from the cleaners the next morning."

"Any other calls coming into that line since?" Nesterov inquired.

"No, sir."

Nesterov thought for an uncomfortable minute, and then got up from his chair. He had a glint in his eye which the men had not seen for quite some time.

"Here is what we are going to do. Andrey, I want you to contact that reporter we had on the payroll from the *Washington Sun*. I want him to make sure that this story gets a lot of attention, and make sure it is written in a way that makes it look better than the *pathetic* job you guys really did. Pavel, I want a thousand copies made of this picture of Freeman's kid."

He paused for an instant and then turned towards Amosov. "Felix, you have the most critical responsibility. I want you to forward the copies of this kid's picture to everybody we know in any family—any syndicate. We need to make this into a nationwide manhunt—something that will bind all of our comrades in the business together. Tracking down and killing the FBI's most important informants will send a hell of a message to any *sooka ebnataya* who thinks the government can protect them."

He paused again, looking over the few men he had left. An uncharacteristic (at least in recent memory) smile slowly emerged from his face. "And get me Mikhail Ostankino on the line."

PHOENIX

iii

Viktor Ilyushenko walked up to his front door having completed a less than pleasant day. He had already medicated himself with a double dose of *Meglatavan*, a nasty habit which he had developed over the years. His driver had taken him through his security gate to his home and then left on an errand which Viktor could not recall.

Not fully retaining all of his faculties, he reached his key out towards his door. Only something was wrong. There was no longer a keyhole. He pondered the situation for a moment.

Where did I leave the blei keyhole? he thought.

After a few moments of reflecting on his dilemma, Viktor realized that his steel storm door had been replaced. It now seemed to be a... a much larger door made of oak.

He stepped back and looked up from where he stood. To his surprise, there was a large knocker on this door. Thoroughly perplexed, he attributed this vision to his heavy dose of the drug. Still, he had never known it to have hallucinatory effects before.

He shrugged his shoulders, decided he must be dreaming, and went along with the game. He stepped up and swung the knocker three times. The door slowly creaked open. Viktor stepped forward, entering into a large, yet unfamiliar, anteroom. He took a few steps forward, when a swift breeze swept past him, closing the door.

Viktor looked around and about himself. He was standing in a castle from somewhere out of the fourteenth or fifteenth century. The inside was dimly lit by large candles and torches situated throughout the halls. He looked up at the magnificent tapestries hanging along the great walls of the anteroom.

As he was admiring the tapestries, a gentle sound of musical bells danced sleepily through the musty air. Viktor turned in the direction of the pleasant reverberation and observed a flickering light, most likely from a roaring fireplace, coming from around the far corridor.

He moved towards the music, which was both sedating and strangely seductive to him. He entered a brightly lit room filled with the tremendous smell of a well-marinated roast. He glanced to his right and saw a cloaked man rotating a roasting pig over a large flame.

From the left, the music continued. Viktor turned to see a small boy, no more than six or seven, playing the xylophone intently. The boy was dressed as a medieval English nobleman. What struck him as odd, however, were the sunglasses the boy wore, serving as a visible paradox while masking the boy's eyes.

Viktor moved closer to the young lad, beginning to feel as if all his senses were at their peak performance. Not wanting to interrupt the boy's playing, he seated himself in the armchair situated directly in front of the child.

The boy completed his piece, and Viktor, unable to restrain himself, clapped his hands vigorously for the performance. The boy looked up at the sedated Ruskie, who continued to smile at him. The boy spoke.

"Oh, hello, Viktor."

Viktor stopped clapping, astonished that the boy knew his name.

"Do... I know you?"

The boy shook his head. *"No, no, I do not think so. Yet still, you are killing me."*

He stared in utter incredulity at the boy. *"Killing you? H-How? I have never met you before..."*

"Haven't you?" the boy questioned smartly, folding his arms.

A shriek erupted from behind him, and Viktor twisted in his chair. He looked in horror as he saw the roasting pig, only it was no longer fully a pig. It had Jesse's face on it.

"Help me Dr. I! He won't let me go! He won't let me go!"

"Do not concern yourself with him!" the boy commanded.

Viktor swung back around towards the boy reactively.

"What are you doing to him?" he shrieked. Yet as he tried to stand from his seat, ghastly hands shot through the fabric of the chair, clasping his wrists and ankles. After a brief, futile struggle, Viktor looked up in terror at the child before him.

"It is my time, and you are in my way, Viktor. I hope you will not take this too personally, though."

Viktor continued to look on, speechless. The boy smiled for the first time.

"Tell me, Dr. Ilyushenko. Have you ever heard the expression 'He who lives by the sword, dies by the sword'?"

PHOENIX

The boy paused for a moment, savoring Viktor's terror. *"To be honest, I really was not too fond of the gentleman who came up with that quote, but I have to admit, it is quite poetic. In fact, I would be so bold as to say that that expression epitomizes 'poetic justice'. Do you not agree?"*

Viktor strained to comprehend what exactly the boy was talking about when he suddenly felt the chair he was in lean back until he was lying flat and looking straight up towards the cathedral ceiling. When Viktor realized what was being lowered from above, he gasped inwardly in preparation of a loud scream. However, at this same instant, a fifth hand sprung forth from the fabric beneath him, covering his mouth.

"Come on, Doc, take it like a man. This won't hurt one bit!"

And then the boy broke into menacing laughter, echoing throughout the room, as the greatly oversized hypodermic needle thrust speedily downward towards the chest of its prey.

18

Washington Sun   ~

THYATIRA, PA — In an apparent retaliation by organized crime leaders, Harold and Violet Freeman were slain in their home earlier this week.

The Freeman family became part of the Federal Bureau of Investigation's Witness Protection Program following Harold Freeman's infiltration of the Caputo organized crime syndicate in the Southwest.

Freeman's activities led to the largest number of convictions against the mafia in this nation's history, and his testimony was the primary factor in the conviction and subsequent execution of mob boss Danny Caputo.

Representatives of the FBI, who spoke under the condition of anonymity, shared that the slaying of the Freeman family will be seen as a major blow in their efforts to secure witnesses to testify against organized crime leaders in the future.

i

Vanya sat in Jonathan's room, continuing to churn away at the synthesizer. She had been doing so, up to twelve hours a day, for nearly a week now. Progress was slow—almost minuscule—but she was determined to get her nephew back.

PHOENIX

She did not play at all the previous day, when she learned that Viktor Ilyushenko had died of a stroke. She wept for him in her own heart but realized that she needed to tend to the living. She had maybe a day or two's sugar solution left for Jonathan's I.V., and she was concerned as to what she would do when that ran out.

While she played on, contemplating this thought, the security guard buzzed in. Vanya instantly froze, the last note from Vivaldi's *Il cimento dell'armonia e dell'invenzione* still ringing in the air. She was not expecting anyone and had no idea as to who could be randomly stopping by.

She gave a brief glance towards Jonathan, who would now move his fingers on occasion. She grabbed her container of holy water, sprinkled it on him in the Sign of the Cross, then quickly crept down the stairs.

"Yes, Solanus?" she inquired into the monitor.

"A friend of Master Jonathan's, ma'am."

She slowly approached the front door, peering through the security peephole. She was pleasantly surprised, and quite a bit relieved, when she saw Nathan standing there next to Solanus with a guitar case in hand. Vanya took a moment to mull over what she would say to him, then buzzed the guard back.

"Of course, Solanus. Send him in."

She waited a moment for Nathan to approach, then opened the door.

"Why, Nathan," Vanya began with a forced smile. "How nice to see you!"

Nathan grinned. "Hi, Mrs. S., I just stopped by to see how Jon was doing. Thought maybe I'd play him a few tunes to lift his spirits."

She tumbled in her mind. *Lift his spirits.* The thought danced in her head for a moment. "Oh, why that's nice of you, Nathan, but Jonathan is really ill and he needs his rest. I would be afraid that—"

"I heard you playing upstairs yourself, Mrs. S.," Nathan interrupted. "So I guess I wasn't the only one thinking that way, huh?"

He was now smiling earnestly, watching as a troubled look came across Vanya's face.

"Mrs. S., are you okay?"

Suddenly and unexpectedly, Vanya burst into tears.

Nathan, stunned by the sudden show of emotion, stepped inside and closed the door. He awkwardly brought his hands up, hugging the mother of his best friend.

"What's wrong, Mrs. S.? What's happened to Jon?"

She sniffled and stepped back, trying to regain her composure. She looked up at Nathan with tearstained eyes, feeling a twinge of embarrassment.

"Oh... oh, I'm sorry, Nathan. It's just been... so... so hard for me. Jonathan has gotten real bad, and I just don't know what to do."

Nathan looked steadily at Mrs. Storm, trying to search for the right word or phrase to say in order to comfort her. "Let... let me help, Mrs. Storm... please. Jon... he's my best friend. Maybe I can help him."

Vanya looked down, choking back the tears, and silently nodded. The two of them moved towards the stairs, then up to Jonathan's room.

Nathan entered the room, attempting to prepare himself for the worst. Still, he was unable to hide his reaction, seeing his friend of many years lying motionless on the bed and hooked up to an I.V.

"Oh my God," he whispered.

"He's been this way for a week," Vanya began, trying to think up a logical story as she went along. "The doctor says it's a coma from... stress. He suggested I play familiar music to try to get a response out of him."

"Has it worked?" Nathan asked, moving slowly towards the seat on the far side of the bed. He kept his gaze locked intently on his friend.

"Some," Vanya responded. "I just play some old classical pieces... something I used to—"

"Play it, please," Nathan looked up helplessly. "If it helps him."

She nodded and sat down at the desk. She began to play *Für Elise*, one of her favorite Beethoven pieces. Nathan kept his eyes fixed upon Jonathan as she played.

Nearly half an hour went by before Nathan saw the index finger on Jonathan's left hand move.

"He moved!" Nathan shrieked.

Vanya jumped, abruptly stopping what she was playing.

"No! No, don't stop. It's working!"

She smiled softly and then resumed her playing.

Nathan continued to watch Jonathan, but then raised his stare slowly, up towards the synthesizer. He listened to the music, really *listened* to it for perhaps the first time since he had been there. After a moment, he leaned over, opened his guitar case, and slipped out the acoustic guitar on which he and Jonathan had been composing together.

He nodded his head to the general rhythm of the melody Mrs. Storm played. Then he slowly entered into the music, gently plucking the strings as Mrs. Storm caressed the keys on the synthesizer.

She looked up towards Nathan, pleasantly surprised. Vanya had never played with an accompaniment before, but the gentle mix of instruments danced softly in her ears.

The duo watched as Jonathan's fingers began to move, a few at a time at first, until all were in motion. As they continued to play, Nathan and Vanya met eyes, both tearing up, both fostering a newly established sense of hope for the tortured soul lying before them.

ii

Eliot Lige sat directly across from Ibn Fatimah, the new Foreign Minister of the Islamic Union. Five meters of solid oak table and two-dozen subordinates separated the two. Both men had spent the first two hours exchanging pleasantries and small talk as cameramen snapped their pictures for the photo opportunity. Both knew each other's positions and intentions weeks prior to the meeting.

As the members of the press were excused from the room, Fatimah stared at Lige, eager to progress with the meeting's main topic. He did not want to appear weak in front of his men, yet he was anxious to prove his worthiness as an international diplomat. Lige, sensing Fatimah's impatience spoke to his interpreter.

"I am grateful for this opportunity to work with you, Minister Fatimah, and I look to many more positive negotiations with you. I feel we have made some good initial steps today, but I would be remiss if I did not admit that there are greater concerns which we will need to address."

Following a moment to hear the translation, Fatimah nodded, almost in relief. "I agree."

Fatimah looked, pondering deeply, around the table at all of his men, who in turn stared back curiously at him. His eyes returned to the Christian Israeli. "Tell me, Minister Lige," he began. "How is your Arabic?"

The translator leaned over towards Lige, who waved him off. Intrigued, he looked at Fatimah. "Not so good," he responded in the young Egyptian's native tongue.

Fatimah surprised all in the room when he laughed, then nodded. "Leave us," he commanded his men. Each looked up at him, their mouths agape. Fatimah's pleased look became stern after a moment of inaction. "Do I need to repeat myself?" he bellowed, which instantly sent his men scurrying.

Lige's interpreter looked at him, and Lige nodded back. The interpreter stood and exited the room with the rest of the men.

When all had vacated the conference room, Fatimah walked over to close the door. He turned back towards Lige with a look of both intrigue and curiosity. "Since when does a Christian from Israel take the time to learn the language of my people?"

Lige responded methodically. "Language has always been a barrier which has kept our people apart; let us hope that our mutual goodwill will be the language which one day brings us together."

Fatimah smiled widely. "You speak the language of diplomacy quite well, my friend, but do you think that will be enough to accomplish the impossible task for which your pompous prime minister has sent you here?"

Lige did not allow the pleasant expression on his face to fade. "With *Elohim*, are not all things possible?"

Fatimah smiled again and nodded. "If nothing else, I believe I will enjoy the poetry of your words. Our good Imam has sent me, a mere boy, to speak with you, a diplomat a few years my senior..."

"Perhaps more than a few," Lige responded with a slight smile.

Fatimah smiled back. "Perhaps. Yet, in truth, I cannot help but think that there is an incredible familiarity about you which I cannot quite place. But for now, let us then talk of peace in hopes that we may prevent what many consider to be an inevitable war."

Lige nodded to the foreign minister, who now moved towards the window, looking out across the Islamic city of Paris. "You know, Minister Lige, I was there the day it happened."

Lige looked curiously at Fatimah. "Sir?"

Fatimah looked back towards him, somewhat surprised. "Come now, Minister Lige, the most significant day of our time. The day the Dome of the Rock crumbled to the ground."

Lige's expression slipped for just for a moment, but he was sure that Fatimah had not caught it. He listened intently as the foreign minister continued.

"Many of my people insist that it was a bomb planted by the Israelis, but I know better." Fatimah paused for a moment, shaking his head. "I was just a child, traveling with my family. We had just completed our pilgrimage to Mecca, and it was then time for the Dome. I found it all quite boring really. But I felt the earth tremble beneath me. Not just once, but twice."

He stopped momentarily, seemingly overcome by emotion. "Though no others would acknowledge it, I heard *music*, just preceding the tremors. I have never forgotten that tune—melodic—enchanting—haunting." He paused, seemingly straining to maintain his composure. "I had never seen my father cry before. But on that day, he could not stop!"

Fatimah took a moment, clearly hindered by interior forces beyond his dominion. He then looked back towards Lige with glistening tears in his eyes, shaking his head. "I do not know how you intend to frame what you came here to propose today, Christian, but if you have the Wisdom of Solomon within you, and you can see a way to navigate this... situation... in a manner which neither nation will lose face, then you are a greater man than I."

Lige paused for a moment, returning an empathetic gaze to the man who had just bared his soul to him.

"Then let this day be remembered as the day when two sons of Abraham met so that they might build a brighter future for their children and their children's children."

Fatimah stared back at him, captivated, while he attempted to hold back the tears of great emotion. He moved to the seat adjacent to this man of ageless wisdom and sat down.

iii

Jake Hanssen hung up the phone in disgust. As Clarence Hoover looked on, Hanssen circled the table and slumped into his seat.

"This is bad for the Bureau. Real bad," he muttered.

Hoover nodded. Losing perhaps their most effective informant in the history of the FBI was bad enough; seeing it plastered on the front of the *Washington Sun* was inconceivable.

"Where the hell were Smithers and Burns that night?" Hoover demanded.

Hanssen shook his head. "God only knows. We still haven't heard from them. For all I care, they can stay gone. We've got worse problems now, like for instance, how are we ever again going to convince a potential informant that we can protect him?"

Hoover did not have an answer to this. The thought had crossed his mind several times already today. He looked back up to Hanssen, who was pacing again.

"What are we going to do about the reporter?" Hoover asked.

"I've already had him picked up for questioning. I'd like to know how he learned about this hit before we did."

Hoover hesitated for a moment, biting his lower lip. "What about the kid?" he questioned.

Hanssen shook his head. "I'm afraid to pull him in right now. Nesterov didn't find Freeman until we relocated him. If he knew where the kid was, he would have taken them both out at the same time when he had the chance." He paused. "No, I'm sure Nesterov doesn't know where the kid is. And I'm not going to risk taking any additional action with him—we may have a leak."

"So how do we tell the kid?"

Hanssen shook his head. "We don't, not unless he contacts us—at least not yet. There is to be no contact with him until I decide it's safe. As of now, you, myself, and Edgar in Pergamum are the only ones who know of his whereabouts." He paused in a moment of contemplation. "No, let's handle this one from the back door. I want Nesterov and his men tracked. If they make the slightest move towards North Carolina, we pull him in. I just hope he isn't one to read the papers."

19

"You must break the outside to let out the inside;
to get at the kernel means breaking the shell.
Even so, to find nature herself,
all likenesses have to be shattered."

– Eckhart

i

Nathan looked wearily at the mother of his best friend, having just completed their version of a Chopin duet. She nodded to him with a look of understanding, and Nathan put his instrument down.

His muscles ached and his fingertips burned. For three days straight he had played with Mrs. Storm – it was clear from where Jonathan's musical genius had come. The process was long and tedious, but seeing his friend move closer and closer to reality with each note made the task well worth the effort.

Mrs. Storm quietly slipped out of the room.

Nathan looked at Jonathan, who was now able to be propped up in bed. He had opened his eyes the day before, but they might as well have still been closed. A blank stare remained on the young man's face.

After a few minutes, Mrs. Storm re-entered the room with a bowl of soup. Jonathan was now able to take liquids, for which they were both eternally grateful. This meant they would no longer have to consider bringing additional outsiders into their predicament.

Nathan looked at Mrs. Storm as she fed Jonathan. He squirmed in his chair as he searched for the manner in which to ask the question that had been sitting in his mind for the past few hours.

"Mrs. Storm?" he managed to get out.

"Yes, Nathan?" she replied, keeping her eyes fixed on Jonathan as she slipped a spoonful of chicken broth into his mouth.

"Do you think that, maybe tomorrow, I could bring Jon over to Simon's house... you know... so we could all play for him?"

She stopped her motion, looking back at Nathan fearfully. "Oh no, Nathan, we can't bring others into this, we—"

"Mrs. S, you saw the difference it made when I started playing with you. It sped up his progress. If we brought in the band, it might bring him out even quicker."

She shook her head and dipped the spoon in for another mouthful for Jonathan. "I'm afraid that's not possible... I don't want others to see Jonathan this way."

But Nathan could sense her resolve crumbling. She knew that what he was saying might very well be true. Jonathan made as much progress in a day with the two of them together as he had in three or four days with her alone.

"How about," he prodded, "I bring the guys over here? We can set up downstairs somewhere—maybe the garage—and just see what happens. The guys won't say anything, I promise. And we'll play the songs back to Jonathan which he wrote, which came from him. I know it would speed things up, I just know it!"

Vanya hesitated, knowing she could not come up with an adequate counter-argument to what Nathan had just offered. She finally conceded, albeit that her reluctance was clear.

"Okay, Nathan. We'll try it... for one day. But I want to speak to the boys first, and if it doesn't make a significant difference really quickly—"

"They're outta here."

ii

Jesse struggled to get a hold of the visions and voices that swept through his head, but he was grateful to no longer be in perpetual darkness. Being fully aware of his consciousness, yet not experiencing one iota of stimuli through any of his senses, was the most terrifying experience of his life.

Then, out of the darkness, he heard the delicate sound of music. It seemed to cut through the eternity of gloom. Though the visions he began to see were far from pleasant, anything was better than the emptiness which had encompassed him earlier.

Though fleeting, the visions grew more vivid over time. Then the music stopped, and Jesse suddenly had the sensation of floating. A haze of crimson red began to focus below him; he realized that he was slowly descending upon a barren landscape of large black rocks scattered among a plane of coarse red sand.

His descent ended with a smooth landing. As his senses sharpened, Jesse became aware of the deathly heat around him. He surveyed the landscape, now recognizing that the black rocks scattered throughout the scene were steaming.

He looked to the left, where an orange glow emanated from behind a sizable range of plateaus, perhaps a kilometer off. As his eyes began to focus, he was able to discern the figure of a man, perhaps halfway between himself and the plateaus, walking away from him. Wiping the newly formed sweat from his forehead, Jesse started in a slow trot towards the figure.

After what seemed like an eternity, the image faded into the rocks. Jesse paused, gasping for breath in the intense heat, and instinctively looked back the way he had come. There, not more than a hundred meters behind him, was a young boy. He was moving towards Jesse, who was now able to make out some of the boy's features.

He looked to be perhaps seven years old and was oddly dressed in a white tuxedo with a top hat to match. As he came closer, Jesse became aware of another oddity. The boy was wearing dark glasses. His smile was now discernable, but Jesse did not sense any warmth behind that grin.

Jesse felt his aching muscles begin to cramp, and a sensation of nausea began to overtake him. The boy moved closer, his grin seemingly growing wider with each step. Jesse watched as a dark spot began to emerge from the center of the boy's chest, slowly expanding. It was only a moment later that it became clear what this was—the boy was bleeding, though whatever the injury, it did not seem to hinder him in the slightest. Jesse swooned for an instant before he was yanked out of his vertigo by a booming voice.

"MOVE!"

Jesse stood upright and looked towards the range of plateaus from which the voice had come. He glanced back towards the boy, who was no longer smiling. The boy had stopped for an instant, then began walking at a quickened pace. His walk turned into a slow jog, and then he broke out into an all-out run towards Jesse.

"Move, Jesse! Now!"

Jesse turned and sprinted towards the hills. He reached them quickly, now able to hear the boy's labored breathing behind him, and did not hesitate to begin his ascent.

"Hurry, Jesse!" the voice anxiously bellowed.

He was now aware of the boy's hands just barely missing him, clawing fanatically from below. As Jesse came within centimeters of the peak, the boy finally grabbed his foot.

Jesse screamed out as he realized the tremendous strength of the boy. He felt his hands begin to slip from the stones which he clung to. The boy's second hand grabbed his calf as Jesse felt himself let go.

Just as he prepared to release a scream, two hands shot over from above the ridge, clasping his. He looked up, astonished to find he was face to face with the man from his past—the one he had come to know as 'Hanoch.'

"You must fight for it, Jesse. Do not let go!"

Jesse struggled, kicking his feet while he heard the boy laughing insanely below, and still clinging on.

"I can't shake him... I can't!" Jesse cried out.

"You must!" Hanoch roared back.

At that instant, Jesse felt one last surge of energy, but just as he began to clear the plateau, he heard a tearing sound.

He looked down, expecting to see that his pants had ripped. But instead what he saw tearing was his... *skin.*

The grotesque tearing sound continued, and an instant later his entire covering of skin ripped from his body, with the subsequent dissipation of the weight of the boy. Jesse looked up to Hanoch, who stared back at him with an expression of confusion and horror.

The last image Jesse saw, out of the corner of his eye, was that of the enigmatic boy falling to the dark abyss below, clinging to his newly acquired skin and laughing uncontrollably.

20

"Weeping," he chanted, "may endure the night. And what shall come with the morning?"

And he answered himself coldly, "A funeral. A funeral."

– Walter Wangerin, Jr.
The Book of Sorrows

i

Simon, Nathan, and Joey each churned away at their respective instruments, watching a catatonic Jonathan sitting slumped in an easy chair they had brought out to the garage. They continually exchanged anxious glances with each other, then hopeful glimpses towards Jonathan, as they played the three songs they had composed together. After an hour of no noticeable response, Nathan finally waved the others off.

Both Joey and Simon stopped immediately, clearly relieved.

"This isn't working, man," Simon started. "I'm telling you, the dude fried his brain on LSD—I've seen it before. Heck I *lived* it. But no music is going pull anyone out of that bad trip. You either snap out or you don't."

Joey remained silent but switched his gaze from Simon to Nathan in anticipation of a response. Nathan continued to observe Jonathan intently. He still possessed the blank stare he had the day before.

"We're playing like crap," Nathan muttered.

"Aww, Nate, I don't think Jon is in any position to critique—"

Nathan shot an angry stare at Simon. "What I'm saying is that we're just playing the notes mechanically, looking at each other and at Jon. That's not what this music's about. It's not just a funky beat that's kind of catchy. It's more of an experience. Remember the magic we felt the day we met Joey and all four of us played together for the first time?"

Both Joey and Simon nodded solemnly. Nathan looked for a moment towards Jonathan, when a seemingly random inspiration hit him. He unstrapped his acoustic guitar, and then moved over towards Jonathan, placing the guitar in his hands. As Joey and Simon looked on in wonder, Nathan wrapped Jonathan's left hand around the neck of the guitar, and placed a pick in his right hand. Kneeling, he looked intently into Jonathan's eyes, which still displayed his blank stare.

"Come on, Jon-boy. We know you're in there, and we just want to do a little jam session, okay? All the guys are here, and we got to start practicing if we're gonna get rich and famous, right? So you just listen for a little bit, okay, buddy? You just listen then jump in whenever you're ready. Okay? Anytime you're ready."

The quaking—and near desperation—in Nathan's voice was evident to his band mates, though at this point he felt he had nothing to lose. He backed away, staring intently at Jonathan, then taking a deep breath, he turned to hook up his electric guitar. "Okay, guys, let's do this. And no slacking off this time. This is the real thing. You all got it?"

Joey and Simon looked at each other and shrugged in agreement.

"All right," Nathan began with a sly smile on his face. *"Heart and Soul* from the top..."

Vanya moved towards the door to the garage with a tray of lemonades for the boys. They had been playing all day, and she could not help tearing up when she thought about the effort they were exerting in an attempt to help Jonathan.

She opened the door in the middle of a song, entering with a smile which immediately evaporated as the platter of drinks fell from her hands. Shards of glass scattered across the garage floor as she stood frozen.

There, in the easy chair on the far side of the room, Jonathan sat playing guitar. Though he still stared blankly, Vanya could now see just the smallest glimpse of life in him.

"Dear Jesus," she gasped.

The three boys, having stopped playing at the sound of shattered glass, grinned proudly back towards Jonathan's mother.

"What… oh my God, oh, Jonny!"

Vanya's instinct was to fly to him with a warm embrace, but fear of upsetting whatever delicate balance had been reached prevented her from doing so. Nathan reached over, switching off the digital recorder, as it was clear there would be a momentary intermission. Jonathan had stopped playing now too.

"How did you? How long has he been…?" Vanya could not get a full sentence out as the tears began streaming down her face.

"I think Jon's a real ham at heart, Mrs. S.," Nathan responded, smiling. "Strangest thing is, the last three songs we played, I've never heard before. Jonathan just started playing a progression on his own, and we just kind of filled in. You were right about a lot of things, Mrs. S. The boy's got music in his soul."

Vanya, overcome with emotion, stood speechless. She looked around at the boys, who smiled eagerly back at her. Finally she was able to speak.

"I'll get some more lemonade."

ii

Menachem Ashir waited anxiously as Eliot Lige entered his office. Lige had informed him ahead of time that an agreement had been reached which was in need of his blessing.

Needless to say, Ashir was astonished by the news, yet at the same time both skeptical and confused, to say the least. What could Lige have possibly pulled off in this no-win situation?

He smiled uncomfortably as Lige sat down with an air of confidence about him.

"It is good to see you, Eliot. I am anxious to hear the terms of the agreement which you have worked out."

Foreign Minister Lige smiled and opened his briefcase, from which he withdrew a single piece of paper. He placed it in front of Ashir.

Ashir looked at the piece of paper for an instant, then glanced back at Lige suspiciously. "What is this?"

Lige nodded, gesturing towards the paper. "Terms of the agreement, awaiting your approval, Prime Minister."

Ashir held Lige's gaze for a moment, then began to read the agreement. A scowl came across his face as he completed the paper.

"What is this—some kind of joke?"

Lige shook his head. "Not at all, Prime Minister, this is an agreement to pronounce that Mount Moriah be declared off-limits to all for the next seven years, while more pressing political matters are hashed out between our nations in a series of quarterly meetings. At the close of the seven years, we will then allow the spiritual leaders of the Islamic, Jewish, and Christian faiths to ascend the Mount. At that time, an agreement will be sealed which will serve all of those who profess faith in the One God for the next millennium."

Ashir stared at Lige angrily. "This is not what I asked for! I will not sign it!"

Lige maintain a serene disposition. "I do not feel, Prime Minister, that that would be a wise choice. This afternoon Foreign Minister Fatimah will announce to the world the terms of this agreement as a step towards a real world peace which has been spoken of for so many centuries past. He will credit you with making the first step. I think you will find that the people of the world have grown weary with the ongoing conflicts in the Middle East and care very little about what temple or shrine gets built where. I feel the nations will be very generous in their support of a peace agreement."

"The Caliph will never accept this either!"

"Though I have no doubt his motives are not benign, he too knows he is not in a position to take on both Israel and the entire U.L.D.N."

"Not yet!"

"Yes, Prime Minister, not yet…"

"This time we give him will allow him to become stronger!"

"With all due respect, sir," Lige began with a cool, yet deliberate tone. "Perhaps we are entering a season where we are best to leave Islam to its own devices. If it is not of *Elohim*, then it will implode upon itself. We must trust that Divine Providence is at work!'

Ashir was livid, but he made a weak attempt to cover his frustration. "You have quite cunningly backed me into a corner. Even if the people of Israel are looking for peace, my opponents will use my failure to rebuild the Jewish Temple against me in the next election!"

"That may be true, Prime Minister. But I think that if you do not endorse this agreement after the Foreign Minster of the Islamic Union announces his desire to do so to the world, you may find the rest of the international community unwilling to continue friendly relations with the Nation of Israel."

Ashir clenched his teeth, staring in a hostile fashion towards Lige. Lige, however, maintained the same look of serenity with which he had entered the room. Finally, Ashir spoke.

"You have won this round, Christian. But from this day forth, you may find this post which you hold to be a very dangerous one."

iii

"I suppose, Father, it would not be a proper statement of faith to say, 'I can't believe it.'"

President Hugh Lang and Father Daniel Ananias watched the television as the Mount Moriah Accord, an agreement between the Nation of Israel and the Islamic Union announced only two days prior, was signed. Father Daniel had traveled to Washington, D.C. to preside over the wedding of Lang's daughter. The witnessing of the historic accord provided a fitting close to a grace-filled week.

Father Daniel smiled. "I have a hard time accepting it as well. It is hard to trust. But I sense there is some legitimate goodwill playing out here, even if that goodwill is not shared by all of the players."

Lang nodded, "So true. But I never underestimate how even the slightest ray of hope can transform people."

At that moment, one of the president's aides stepped into the room, setting a binder on Lang's desk. "The weekly mud report, Mr. President."

"Thank you, Szandor."

The aide exited the room as President Lang opened the binder and began to scan the report. A somewhat amused expression came across his face.

"The 'mud report'?" Father Daniel inquired.

President Lang looked up. "Ahh… yes, Father. I get a weekly report on the supposed mud that has been brought up on me or my family. According to the latest rumor mill, it seems that, during their time of missionary work in Iraq, my parents were actually in league with the Kurdish rebels, coordinating several terrorist-like attacks on the legitimate Iraqi authorities. Additionally, it seems my father was personally responsible for ordering the hanging of a Turk who had been captured during an incursion."

Father Daniel looked dismayed. His rescue by the Lang family was never out of the forefront of his mind. "This is terrible! How could they fabricate such a thing?"

The president shrugged. "The first, and most effective, manner of undermining my administration and its policies is to distract and discredit. These reports have me in everything from affairs with prostitutes to molesting children to being a secret foreign Islamic agent… this last one of course, due to my birth in the Middle East when my parents were missionaries in Saudi Arabia."

"It does not seem that any of these have been able to stick."

"No, not yet. But to be honest, Father, it wouldn't be the worst thing if some of them lingered a bit."

Father Daniel looked confused. "I do not understand how, in the good Lord's name, such slander would be acceptable—or even desirable."

The president paused a moment, making sure no one was in earshot of their conversation. The few who remained in the room were plastered to the television, which was now showing Ministers Lige and Fatimah shaking hands.

"You see Father, if a few of these linger, it buys me time… because those that oppose me will wait to see if they gain traction, thinking perhaps this could become the 'big scandal' that cripples my administration. But if they find too quickly that the attempts at discrediting me are failing, they will have no choice—in their minds—but to move towards more drastic measures…"

iv

Vanya slept for perhaps the first night in weeks. Jonathan had made incredible progress in the past three days. A phone call earlier that evening with her mother revealed that a possible agreement between her father and his rivals in "the business" was imminent. Good things seemed to be falling into place. However, as Vanya began to drift off into the silent abyss of her dreams, she quickly became aware that this would not be a night of restful sleep.

She felt a sudden rush as she was propelled through the blackness into an immense wave of light. She shielded her eyes for a moment with her hands and then opened them, only to find herself standing at the entrance to a great Basilica.

Vanya could see the priest at the far end of the church, standing in front of the altar and beckoning to her. She became aware of a presence next to her, and turned to see the once well-dressed man from her previous visions. Yet here, in this dream, he was dressed in sackcloth. He did not speak to her, but gently took her arm, leading her forward towards the cleric on the dais. Vanya looked about the Basilica as she walked and saw that no one else was in attendance save a woman in black kneeling in the front pew.

As Vanya approached the cleric, she saw that his vestments actually identified him as a deacon. He was young—far younger than one she could have expected to be an ordained minister—a light-skinned African-American with emerald-green eyes. Her eyes wandered to his right, and her face lit up as she recognized the solemn altar boy standing next to him.

"Tobias!"

Vanya tried to spring forward, but the stately man's grip on her arm, though gentle, did not heed. She gave him a look of desperation, but then came to realize that Tobias was not showing any signs of recognizing of her.

Vanya broke her gaze from her nephew, returning to the deacon, now only five steps away. From the east entrance, a man emerged whom she instantly recognized as the once disheveled man from her dreams—and the one who had saved Jesse many years ago. He too was dressed in sackcloth.

The deacon held up his thumb and forefinger before her and whispered, *"Body of Christ."*

The accent of the deacon was unusual, sounding possibly Cajun or Creole. Vanya looked confused, as she did not see anything in his fingers. She looked down at Tobias, who returned her gaze. Turning back towards the deacon, she held her cupped hands out, responding, *"Amen."*

The deacon then placed a tiny mustard seed in her palm. Vanya was about to inquire as to the meaning of this when she heard a familiar voice from behind her.

"Protect the seed, and you will offer salvation to the Body."

She turned to see that the kneeling woman in black was none other than her sister, Marisha. Marisha did not look up but continued to pray with her eyes closed.

"I do not understand," Vanya interjected.

Marisha did not change her position but continued to speak.

"There are things which you cannot comprehend which must come to pass. For now, you must protect the seed. All is not as it should be, and this is our only hope."

Vanya looked back down at the mustard seed, which now pulsated in her palm. She heard music as she began to feel lightheaded. Turning again, she looked down upon Tobias. The surreal nature of the vision deepened as, from behind the altar, a tree began to sprout up. All other aspects of the scene began to melt away until she and Tobias were standing in the familiar clearing where the tree upon the grassy knoll stood.

She again looked to Tobias, whose eyes dropped to the ground. He turned solemnly and began to saunter towards the tree, stopping only momentarily at the three graves. Vanya felt herself unable to budge as her nephew resumed his movement, reaching the enigmatic tree which had always invoked conflicting feelings of peace and foreboding within her. Tobias looked back, and Vanya saw to her dismay a spot of blood appear in the center of his chest, rapidly soaking through his cassock. He gazed at her with an expression that appeared to be one of disappointment, yet mitigated by a twinge of... *confusion?*

The sound of wind chimes emerged as Tobias turned from her and struck the tree with his fist. Vanya's world suddenly began to spin, and then her consciousness faded into another dream.

21

"To me the meanest flower that blows can give
Thoughts that do often lie too deep for tears."

– William Wordsworth

i

It was three a.m. when Vanya awoke from her fitful sleep, somehow having the instinct to check in on Jonathan. Forty-five minutes later, a frightened Vanya held open her front door as Simon and Joey entered, expressions of concern looming on their faces. She nodded to Solanus, who stood faithful watch in the driving rain.

"We got here as quickly as we could, Mrs. S. Have you called the police?"

She nodded, trying to contain herself. "Yes, they said they couldn't take a missing person's report until someone had been gone for more than twenty-four hours." She hesitated, then gestured towards the kitchen. "Please come in and sit down, I've made coffee." Vanya looked again for a moment, then asked, "Where's Nathan?"

The boys exchanged glances. "We aren't sure," Simon responded. "He wasn't at the house."

She paused for a moment, wondering briefly if there was a connection, and then motioned for the two to move towards the kitchen. They did as Vanya instructed and were soon seated at the kitchen table sipping away at piping hot cups of coffee.

"Do you have any idea where Jonathan might have gone?" she asked the boys. "I mean, did anything unusual happen this morning when you all played together?"

Simon and Joey looked at each other. After a moment, Simon spoke.

"To be honest with you, Mrs. S., our sessions have been nothing *but* unusual. I mean... today we just completed composing our seventh new song. And though he hasn't said a word, Jonathan is the one who has done almost all the composing. It's like... like one of those autistic savant things."

Joey looked at Simon, deep in thought. "You know, Si, I really didn't say anything at the time because I thought my mind was playing tricks with me since I was tired. But twice while we were playing that final piece... twice I could have sworn that when I looked at Jonathan, he *winked* at me."

Simon looked wide-eyed at Joey, while Vanya maintained a puzzled expression.

"I thought I saw the same thing," Simon stated.

Vanya looked at the boys in a troubled fashion. "So what does this all mean?"

As Simon opened his mouth to speak, from the next room came the sound of the ringing phone.

ii

Jonathan sat in the clearing in the center of Goodman Forest, meditating. He allowed his mind to wander freely, now confident that he could call it back when he needed to. The world wheeled around him, and he was again atop the mystic plateau overlooking the nations of the Earth.

Luther stood before him, a diabolic grin resting comfortably on his face. *"You have come back to me, my son. Are you now prepared to fulfill your destiny?"*

Jesse stood from the spot where he had been sitting. *"Yes, Father. Yes, I am. But I have learned that my true destiny does not rest in your hands, but in God's... my* true *Father."*

Luther winced, obviously expecting nothing like this. Quickly composing himself, he aggressively stepped forward, responding angrily. *"What is this blasphemy you speak? You are* my *son! You know this to be true - and you* must *follow me! I command you!"*

"No father," Jesse responded serenely. *"You command only those who allow you to. I have grown stronger and can no longer be swayed by your deceptions. I am closing the door to this plane of existence. Goodbye, Father."*

PHOENIX

"No! You cannot betray me! I will see you destroyed first. I—"

But Jesse was already allowing the surreal scene to fade. He had found peace within himself, but he still could not prevent Luther's final words from echoing throughout his mind.

"You are my son..."

iii

Nathan crouched in the corner of the phone booth, the receiver still hanging down by his face. A recorded message stated that he needed to return the receiver to its proper resting place. The rain beat down on the booth, but Nathan could not hear it.

He had received a text message, after which he instantly knew something was wrong. He went to a designated phone booth, per his previous instructions.

"Nathan, I have some bad news..."

He could not get that opening phrase out of his mind. He shivered but was unable to cry. He still could not believe that his parents were gone.

A million thoughts passed through his head. He was alone now. He had nobody. Nathan allowed a brief, even appealing, thought of suicide to wander through his mind. However, the keen sense of survival which he had developed over the years quickly squashed it out. He would have to go on. He could not let anybody know he was hurting. He would have to stay alive so that one day he might avenge the death of his parents.

But what could he do now? He had nobody to talk to, no one who would understand. No one to comfort him.

No one.

Except....

iv

Alexandre Nesterov sat at the head of the table, watching as the heads of seven other syndicates dug into the home-cooked meal which his wife, the elegant Annie D., had prepared for them. Nesterov was pleased at the show of unity amongst the major associations of organized crime.

Felix Amosov, seated at his right, leaned over towards him. "Alex, I have got to hand it to you, you have really turned this entire thing around. Even Logiarato is stuffing his fat face over there."

Nesterov looked down at the far end of the table and held up his wine glass to Mikey Logiarato. Logiarato was the crime boss of the largest syndicate in the northeast, and he was a good man to have on one's side. Still, there was someone missing that would have made the scene complete.

The forever-loyal Andrey Gavrilenkov poked his head into the room, motioning to Amosov, who excused himself and exited the room. A few minutes later he re-entered with a pleased expression on his face.

"Excuse me, gentleman," he announced. "But we will be having one more joining us for dinner."

Nesterov stood as Mikhail Ostankino entered the room. Their eyes met for one apprehensive moment, and then Nesterov slowly made his way to the entrance where his former underling stood. The near-middle-aged Ostankino had finally ditched the bleached-blond American-wanna-be look, though his smoking habit was clearly still intact. He looked, for the first time, like a son of the Motherland.

In a moment they were face to face, both at a loss as to what to say. Finally, Ostankino spoke. "It is... good to see you, Alexandre."

Nesterov narrowed his eyes for an instant, unsure of how to handle Ostankino referring to him by his first name. Was this the man who had given the order to have his son, Yerik, executed? Though no one had ever claimed responsibility, how could it not have been retaliation for the death of Danny Caputo, Mikhail's benefactor? Nesterov had played out this moment over and over in his mind for the past several months, but he was resolved that now was not the time. For now, it would be a pass. By an act of the will, his expression eased. "And you, my old comrade."

A brief, awkward moment passed, and finally the men embraced. Spontaneous applause erupted throughout the room. Things were on the upswing, and Nesterov knew he would need to prepare for this new era that was about to dawn upon them all.

22

"One and the same thing can at the same time be good, bad, and indifferent, *e.g.* music is good to the melancholy, bad to those who mourn, and neither good nor bad to the deaf."

– Benedict Spinoza
Ethics, Part IV, Preface

i

"He wanted us to meet him here?" Joey Escario asked as he, Simon, and Nathan drove up to a small building with a sign identifying it as 'Gnathion Recording Studio'.

"Dang!" Simon responded excitedly. "Jonathan's definitely not one for patience!"

Nathan remained silent, though he could not help but recognize a small seed of hope regaining ground within him.

The entire crew had been waiting for this day, following Jonathan's mysterious phone call a few hours prior to daybreak the night he had gone missing. Preceding his call by not more than five minutes was another bizarre caller who spewed obscenities in an uncontrolled rage before Vanya was able to slam the receiver down.

Jonathan had assured Vanya, Simon, and Joey that he was okay—perhaps even more than okay. The sound of his voice made it clear that every last vestige of whatever held him in the catatonic state had been eradicated. The boys were informed that he needed a few days to get some final things in order, and that he would be in contact soon. That highly anticipated call came only an hour ago.

Simon parked his uncle's van, with the emblem of 'Garf Auto' on both sides, and the three got out. It was still early in the morning. They moved towards the back of the van to begin unloading when Jonathan emerged from the entrance of the studio.

"Hey there, band mates!" he erupted cheerfully.

The three of them looked up, letting their mouths drop. Jonathan moved towards them smiling, his sleeveless shirt exposing a newly crafted tattoo on his left shoulder. Also catching their eye was the cross dangling from his left earlobe.

"What in God's name...?"

"Exactly!" Jonathan responded. The group instinctively hugged each other, and after the alpha-male pleasantries were exchanged, Joey spoke up.

"How did you get us recording time in there?" he inquired.

"Well, in all honesty, they approached me. Apparently it was my grandfather's way of giving me a gift he knew I wouldn't send back."

"Mmm, must be nice having such a cool grandfather," Nathan muttered, attempting to maintain a pleasant front, though knowing that much *unpleasantness* was still brewing inside of him.

Jonathan looked back at him evenly. "He's a lot of things, but 'cool' is not one of them."

Simon then jumped into the conversation. "So how much time we got in there?"

"Twelve hours. Should be more than enough to cut our ten demos."

Joey looked back at Jonathan, doubtfully. "You expect to cut ten demos in one day? Right!"

Jonathan smiled, nodding. "I feel magic in the air, gentlemen!"

Simon and Joey shook their heads, chuckling. "I still say he fried his brain on LSD," Simon exclaimed.

Joey continued to smile. "So what's with the tattoo, Jon? Is that some sort of bird or something?"

Jonathan nodded. "Yes, sir. That there is the mythological bird known as the Phoenix, which, by the way, is the name we're playing under."

Joey made a face. "You named us after a bird?"

Simon shook his head as he unloaded his synthesizer. "Anybody asks me, I'll stick with the idea that it's from the city in Arizona!"

Jonathan looked to Nathan, who appeared to be in a daze. "You okay, Nate?"

Nathan moved his gaze slowly to Jonathan's eyes. "Oh yeah... sure, I'm fine."

"Well," Jonathan chimed in. "Let's make some magic."

To all of their surprise, the band finished recording in only seven hours. The mix-down process took another four and a half. As they listened to the playback of their final song, the boys all leaned back with expressions of both amazement and quiet satisfaction resting on their faces.

"Incredible!" Simon exclaimed. "Like nothing else I've heard. Where did you come up with those wild lyrics, Jon?"

Jonathan shrugged.

"Sounds to me a lot like that screwed-up poetry you're always writing," Nathan groaned, still struggling with the ebb and flow of conflicting emotions within him. Yet the seed of hope was growing. "I'm just glad little drummer boy here was finally able to keep up."

Joey flashed an expression of irritation at Nathan. *Why does he always have to make a stupid-ass comment about me?*

The moment evaporated when Aleister, the production manager, entered the room, handing Jonathan a copy of their digital disc.

"Sounds terrific, guys. It's nice to hear something mixing old and new." He looked down at the music disc Jonathan was now holding. "You know, if you guys are interested, I know someone in the music industry who may be looking for this kind of sound. Would it be okay if I forwarded one of your demo discs to him?"

The boys all looked at each other in disbelief. Jonathan did not miss a beat.

"Is the Pope Catholic?"

ii

"You have failed in your attempt to win over the Chardin boy. You have been given ample time. We cannot wait any longer."

Luther glared back obstinately at the *Illumini* called Marius. Though he refused to admit defeat, he was well aware of the fact that Jesse would not choose to join him of his own free will—not *yet* at least—but time had run out.

"No, my brothers, it is not I who have failed, but the boy. He has failed his birthright, and he has failed his own destiny." Luther clasped his arms behind his back. "I concur, we cannot wait any longer. I had believed that our Master had a purpose in mind for the young boy when He spared his life twelve years ago. But the day has come where I must annihilate what I have brought into this world."

The *Illumini* called Cato addressed Luther.

"You must destroy the seed before the next cycle comes to pass. Until then, we will await your bidding."

"Very well, my brothers. This is but an inconsequential delay in our plans. Though I would have preferred the trail of lesser resistance, the Great Seraph will permit us to take what is rightfully ours."

There was a long pause in the room, and Luther sensed there was still a question in the air.

"Speak, my brothers," he commanded. "There will be no secrets among us."

With only a moment's delay, the *Illumini* called Anaxagoras posed the question. "With the Chardin boy eliminated, who then will serve as the Anointed?"

Luther released his hands from behind his back and moved onto the pentagram in the center of the floor, seeming to be analyzing it intently. He looked up to the *Illumini* with an expression that most closely resembled one of savage lust.

"I have sons other than he..."

iii

"Merry Christmas... *Auntie*."

Vanya was caught off-guard as she navigated the aisles of the department store, seeking some last-minute gifts. Despite the convenience of a nearly empty mall the night before the holiday, it was disheartening that so few now celebrated the birth of the One she knew as Savior.

PHOENIX

A boy who appeared to be Jonathan's age stood before her, smiling wryly.

"I-I'm sorry, do I know you?" she inquired of the young man.

The boy continued to smile. "Don't I look familiar to you, Auntie Vanya?"

He knew her name. And the truth be known, he *did* have a touch of familiarity about him. Yet Vanya was keen enough not to let on, considering the circumstances she had been through over the years.

"I'm afraid I don't, and I'm not exactly sure how you know my name and why you insist on calling me 'Auntie'."

She tried to move past him with her cart, but he stepped in front of her, blocking her way.

"I'm sorry, I really should have introduced myself first. My mother says I tend to be a bit on the rude side. My name is Samuel."

He reached out his hand, and Vanya reluctantly shook it. His familiarity was beginning to grow, but in a very unsettling manner.

"I really wanted to talk to you just a bit about *family*, if I might."

Vanya took a moment to look around her. There were a few other patrons in the store, but they did not seem to be taking notice of her and this boy. The boy used the word 'family' in a way reminiscent of her father and his associates.

The boy called Samuel continued. "You see, I've always wanted a family, you know, a *real* family. I grew up never knowing my father, and my mother was an only child who said her parents were not very nice people. So it was pretty much just me and her our whole lives, moving from here to there, shacking up with the flavor of the month, you know? Well, that changed a bit when we met my piece-of-shit alcoholic stepfather. Then again, what do you expect from a Ruskie?"

Vanya again looked uncomfortably around her. The boy's voice was raising, but still no one seemed to be taking notice.

"But really, I couldn't expect anyone with any sense at all to marry a woman like my mother. She's a... well.... she's a bitch. Marrying a guy that's closer to my age than hers is a bit embarrassing, I might add, but what can you do? Still, she *is* my mother, and like I said, I *really* want a family." He twitched slightly, as if some unseen force had swept through him, then continued. "I'm sorry, I can tend to be a bit tangential as well—racing thoughts in my mind all the time. So where was I? Oh yes! I was getting to the point! So, about six months ago, while in a drunken tantrum, this bum of a father tells me that my mom not only knows the whereabouts of my father, but that I have a *brother.*"

Why isn't anybody noticing us? Vanya reflected anxiously as the level of the boy's voice continued to rise. Samuel did not stop.

"Well, it took a little bit of... *encouragement* to get it out of my mom, but I found out that, as much as she hated my father, for years after I was born, she still tracked him." Then, leaning forward and giving a wink, Samuel whispered, "Personally, I think she's still in love with the man, though she'd never admit it." He leaned back, resuming his loud tone. "But anyway, my real father... well, I don't know. Yes, I've found him, but... he... he gives me mixed messages, you know?"

Vanya felt her heart begin to race. She was sensing something very wrong within this boy. A certain, if not familiar, *presence...*

"So, it seems now, if I wanted any sort of family, I need to approach it from the *fraternal* aspect. It was interesting, but once I knew this brother existed, all of the sudden, I found that I had a sense of where to look for him. You see, Auntie, I've always had this ability... an ability to just *know* things. Do you understand what I'm talking about?"

"I'm afraid I don't."

Samuel shrugged. "Well, for instance, I know that you and your late husband, Gaetano, weren't exactly childless. You had a stillborn son— conceived before you were married, by the way—whom you named Thomas. But it was so painful that you never spoke of it within your family again."

Vanya's eyes widened. "How do you know—?"

"As I said," Samuel interrupted, almost yelling. "I just *know* things. So I followed my senses, did a little detective work, and drew out my brother. It wasn't that hard. I know he calls you 'mom', but you and I know that's a sham, don't we, Auntie?"

The entire scene suddenly grew silent. Vanya darted her eyes, looking for a possible exit from this surreal situation. But she now saw that not only were the people within earshot not paying attention to them, now *everything* around the pair was completely frozen in place.

Samuel shook his head. "I'm sorry, Auntie, people can be so *distracting* at times. So again, where was I? Oh yes, my brother, or half-brother at least, but to me, a brother's a brother. Well, I have to say it is a bit strange, perhaps even disappointing, that Father seems to have a *real* interest in him. I just wish... I just wish he would take notice of *me*. I have many useful abilities too."

"What do you want from me?" the now terrified Vanya whispered.

Samuel smiled and chuckled incredulously. "Haven't you been listening, Auntie? Yes, I know you're not technically my aunt—maybe fraternal aunt once removed... I don't know, relationships are so confusing. But here's the bottom line, as they say; I just want to have family. I just want to belong. Is that so wrong? Could you possibly find it within you to think of me as your very own... nephew?"

Dear Lord, Jesus, protect me from whatever spirit that I sense before me...

Samuel blinked, and suddenly all about them was in motion again. The hold released, Vanya stepped away from her cart and hastened to the exit door.

"Don't worry, Auntie," Samuel called out from behind her, this time clearly audible to the rest of the people in the store. "Your secret's safe with me! I just want family..."

23

The fish looks eagerly at the red fly
With which the fisherman will take him;
But it does not see the hook-
So it is with the poison of the world
Its danger is not realized.

– Mechthild of Magdeburg

i

"They're playing us! They're playing us!" Joey Escario was unable to contain his delight. He burst into the room where Nathan and Jonathan sat, excitedly displaying his portable radio.

Simon came into the room. "What station?" he asked insistently.

"92.7," Joey responded excitedly.

Simon moved over to his audio system and switched to the channel Joey had identified. An air of exhilaration filled the entire room as they heard their song *Personal Demon* across the radio waves.

Minutes later the song completed, a new one followed, and Simon calmly shut off the system. They all sat mesmerized. Joey was the first to interrupt the silence.

"We're really gonna make it, aren't we?"

Nathan gave a somewhat condescending look to Joey. "Easy there, Mr. Judas Priest, this isn't exactly MTV."

"Hey, don't burst the kid's bubble," Simon cut in. "Who knows where this could go?"

"I'm just saying that it's too early to—"

PHOENIX

At that moment the phone rang. Simon got up and moved towards it. "Pessimism never got anyone anywhere."

"Optimism is only for those who have the luxury of living in a bubble," Nathan retorted.

Ignoring the statement, Simon picked up the phone. "Hello?"

Jonathan and Nathan looked at Simon, who now had a queer look on his face. "Yes, he is here. May I ask who's calling?"

Simon's eyes widened as he handed the phone to Jonathan.

Jonathan looked at Simon curiously, then put the phone up to his ear. "Hello?"

"Hello, this is Esau LaVey of Bacchus Records. Am I speaking to a Mr. Jonathan C. Storm?"

"Yes, sir."

"Well, Mr. Storm, I hope you and your buddies are ringing in the New Year in good form."

Jonathan looked at the mostly empty Chinese take-out containers strewn across the coffee table and a couple of warming beers. Not much of a party.

"Ahhh, yes, sir. As best as we can."

"Good to hear that. Listen, a friend of mine forwarded a demo disc of your band to me, and I was intrigued by what I heard. Getting straight to the point, I have been charged with signing one more group in the next three weeks. I was pretty close to closing a deal with a gentleman by the name of Jimi T. Expo when I came across your disc."

"Y-You liked our music?"

"I said I was *intrigued* by it, Mr. Storm. But time is tight right now. I'd like to come out to one of your gigs in the next few weeks so that I can make a final decision."

Jonathan looked over towards Nathan, apprehensively. "You want to see us in concert? Well sir, we don't—"

Nathan's eyes nearly popped out of his head as he grabbed for the phone from Jonathan.

"Hello, sir? Yes. This is ahh... Jim Evans, I'm the band's manager. Please excuse Jonathan. He's a composer, but not the best with logistics. You

157

said you'd like to hear the boys perform?"

The others looked skeptically at Nathan as he listened for a moment.

"Well of course," Nathan responded to the hitherto unknown request. "We would love to have you as our personal guests at one of our upcoming gigs. Ahh…at the Rhine Music Hall."

A brief pause.

"When? Well the date's not finalized yet but… yes, sir, it will definitely be within the next three weeks. If you could leave your number, I'll have my secretary confirm the date and send you the tickets."

Nathan motioned hurriedly for a pen and paper. Simon grabbed a magazine and pencil, shoving it into Nathan's hands. He immediately scribbled down a number.

"Okay, thank you, ahhh… yes, Mr… oh yes, Mr. LaVey… we'll be in touch. Have a good day. Good bye."

He hung up the phone smiling, then instantly became aware that the others were all staring at him.

"What?" he said, holding out his palms.

Jonathan shook his head. "What did you just do… *Jim*? We don't have a gig at the Rhine."

"No, not yet, but that shouldn't be too hard, it's off season. Simon, you've played there before, haven't you?"

"As part of an orchestra, yes, but—"

"Well, I'm sure you have some contacts there. See what you can get us."

Jonathan still was staring at Nathan in disbelief. "Nate, the place holds over three thousand people. How are we going to fill a place like that? Why didn't you just say one of the local bars?"

"Because this is not bar music, Jon!" Nathan retorted. "This is more like a symphony. We would not get a good response in a bar from a bunch of drunks! But we could really show this LaVey our marketability by packing in the Rhine!"

Joey watched on silently as the argument continued.

"Earth to Nathan," it was Jonathan's ball. "How are we going to get three thousand people to come to a concert of someone they don't know and which hasn't even been arranged yet?"

Nathan contemplated this thought for a moment, then his expression became ignited again as an inspirational thought passed through his mind. "We'll make it a charity event... for the soup kitchen! Get the Rhine to donate the theater for the night and charge a few bucks a head!"

At this point, Joey was no longer able to control himself and jumped into the melee. "Yeah! And we can advertise on the radio for free, as a public service announcement!"

Jonathan cocked an eyebrow. It was clear the tide was starting to turn.

Could this really be happening? he thought. He looked cautiously at Nathan. "I suppose I could run off a couple of thousand flyers to distribute."

"That's the spirit!" Nathan responded.

"So much for Mr. Pessimism," Simon joked. "Well, I'll get to work on landing us the place. I'd say we might have a shot."

They all smiled at each other, then Jonathan lifted his beer. "To The Phoenix!"

"The Phoenix!" they exclaimed in unison.

ii

Vanya tried the number for the twentieth time that day, and probably the hundredth time that week. Still no answer. It frightened her not being able to get a hold of her father. Despite the supposed "goodwill" that had been re-established between he and his associates, he was once again in hiding due to the very public murders of the Freeman family and the FBI's subsequent frantic crackdown. Strangely enough, Vanya had learned of this not from her family, but from a news report on a department store television. She had gone through periods of "radio silence" with her family before, but this was not the best timing.

Despite the recent strides towards health and normalcy, Vanya had developed a newfound sense of fear for Jonathan following the encounter with the boy called Samuel. Her recurring dreams also provided a sense of urgency and foreboding. They had returned in a different form each night for the past week, yet they always ended with the bleeding Tobias at that tree. Just a little more that a week ago everything had seemed to be going so right—now, it seemed that payment was due.

A reprieve Lord... could you not grant a reprieve?

Yet Heaven remained silent to her, not so different from her father and mother at this point. Vanya had learned over the years to trust her instincts—or perhaps better put, her intuition. At this time, evil was close; so close she could almost taste it.

She had finally decided to write a letter and mail it to the post office box that her father had wisely obtained months ago. It was her fail-safe method for getting him if all else faltered.

She quickly scribbled out the message:

> Father,
>
> Please come quickly. I think we are in danger here.
> Need help.
>
> > Love, Vanya

She popped the note into the envelope, scribbled out the address, and hastened to the mailbox.

iii

This was it.

Samuel had been summoned earlier that day by one of his father's lackeys. To his own excitement, it was evident that Luther had actually been tracking *him* this time. Despite his father's previously perceived disinterested disposition towards him—a true disappointment to Samuel once his father had learned of his existence—he was now at least intrigued enough by his son to check up on his activities.

"You must be ready to move on a moment's notice," the lackey had said. "It will not be long now."

Perhaps Luther had discovered one of his son's many creative ventures and saw now more clearly how he could be of service to "the cause." Perhaps he realized that the synergy of a father-son team could be a force to be reckoned with. Perhaps he had finally given up on the uninterested, and ungrateful, Jesse.

No matter. Samuel sensed that he now had a date with destiny, and things would never be the same.

24

The Swan Song of Islam?

Excerpted from NewsWatch Magazine

In a recent interview with King Cyrul, the leader of the Kurdish State of Iraq had some interesting, and no doubt controversial, things to say about his former faith.

"Islam is set to die a slow death," the King-without-a-country declared. "The Islamic religion was poised to die at the beginning of the 20th century, then with the development of the combustion engine, and the discovery that the Arab nations were sitting on an ocean of oil, a resurgence took place. It then became a well-funded religion, and with the re-establishment of Israel, Islam also had the benefit of a common enemy which became a unifying force."

Cyrul shared that the power that OPEC, mostly comprised of Islamic nations, was able to yield for many years was most evident in the "Oil Cessation Initiative" more than a decade ago. "There is no doubt in my mind," the sovereign stated, "that OPEC's ceasing of all sales of oil to the United States was in direct response to America's handling of the Philadelphia dirty-bomb incident. The Islamic nations would not allow a resurgence in the then defunct 'War on Terror', and so they cut the lifeblood to the oil-addicted nation."

The king's words here are all too true. Once supply was cut, the price of gasoline in the United States rose eight-fold. "Economic collapse was then inevitable," he shared. "This was the height of Islamic power in the world. Truly passing the so-called 'Golden Years' in influence."

So why now, especially following the Islamic Revolution, where Islam now counts four billion among its followers, would any fool suggest the followers of Mohammed are on their way out?

"Two reasons: God and oil," King Cyrul responds. "The recent technological breakthrough in the United States will allow the mass production of low-cost, ultra-efficient hydrogen automobiles and jets. This will drop the world demand for oil by nearly two thirds in only seven years... though we are already seeing the prices of a barrel of oil plummet." The sovereign added soberly, "Add to that the recent tapping by the United States of huge oil reserves in both the Gulf of Mexico and Alaska, the U.S. is poised to become not only self-sufficient, but even an oil exporter.

> "With the United States establishing world dominance in energy market, it seems 'the Great Satan' is now set to rise from its ashes. Also not boding well for the more radical forms of Islam."
>
> So what will come of Eurabia and the rest of the Islamic Union? "The quality of living in Islamic countries, already weak, will worsen. And then, even the 'Great Imam' will not be able to quell the counter-revolution of starving people."
>
> And what of God? "As a convert to Chaldean Catholicism, I am not afraid to say that Islam is not the religion of God. At best, it is a manmade opportunistic system. At worst... well, it should not take too much imagination to deduce my thoughts on this."
>
> "The only thing, at this point, that can prevent the decline of Islam is Israel itself. Hatred of Israel is still a powerful unifying force among Muslims. If Israel chooses to further incite the Islamic Union, then we may see a very different scenario. It is true, hatred trumps economics.... but not God!"

i

Vanya sat in the back of the stretch limousine which had picked her up from her house several hours earlier. The past two weeks had been a living hell. The once-catatonic Jonathan had been brought back to her, no doubt. Yet in some strange way, she felt she was again losing him.

He barely spent any time at home anymore, since the prospect of this benefit concert had emerged. Coming in at the earlier hours of the morning, sleeping a few hours, then leaving again, claiming with a less and less convincing wink that he had to practice. She had always prayed that Jonathan might find the healing power in song, but it seemed that it had become a downright obsession for him. When she protested, Jonathan would just smile at her.

"It's what I was meant to do... I can feel it!"

"It's too much, Jonathan," she would plead. *"And with this concert... what if he finds us?"*

Jonathan would frown at this point. *"He has no power over me."* And that would be it.

Vanya was eternally grateful when she received the call from her father earlier this morning. Though her mother had brought her father somewhat up to speed during their call the month prior, Vanya filled him in as much as possible on more recent events, including Jonathan's newly acquired evasiveness, and now the public concert which was being held this night. Her father had tried to calm and reassure her, but even he was unable to mask the trace of concern in his voice. So he agreed to fly down with a contingent of men for "additional security" at the concert.

The limousine pulled up to the side tarmac of the Wilmington International Airport, and a fairly large entourage of men led Alexandre and Annie D. Nesterov over to the vehicle. One man held the door open, while another got in, followed by her mother, then father, followed by another man. Mother and daughter embraced.

"My God, Vanya, you look different! You put on a wee bit of weight! You suit it though, love."

Vanya rolled her eyes but could not suppress the tears. Yes, this was the same Irish Catholic mother that never recognized that she had made it to adulthood.

Next, father and daughter embraced.

"Vanya, it is so good to see you." Nesterov became teary eyed for a moment himself but quickly pulled it together, not wanting to appear weak in front of some of his newly acquired men.

Vanya was silent, clinging to a childish sense of relief at seeing her parents. As the limousine began to pull away, she saw two other vehicles full of men pull out with them.

Following her eyes, Nesterov responded. "Just a precaution, dear Vanya. We have built the foundation of a great, yet still fragile, empire. I have two other cars meeting us tonight, as added security for Jesse."

"*Jonathan*," Vanya reminded him.

ii

The boys pulled up to the Rhine Music Hall in Simon's van (now affectionately dubbed "the Garf-mobile" by Nathan), easily finding a close parking spot in the pothole-ridden parking lot. Nathan was the first to hop out, staring up at the structure in which they would be playing in less than three hours. He raised his hands, exclaiming, "Welcome to the jungle!"

Simon and Joey emerged next, smiling at Nathan's antics. Jonathan was the last one out, already seemingly in a dream. He looked up at the music hall with an expression of such intensity and emotion that the others could not help but stop and look at him.

He spoke to them without diverting his gaze. "LaVey should be here to meet with us in about a half-hour. Let's go take a look."

The remaining three nodded, falling in behind Jonathan as he moved towards the building. Nathan, however, held his arm out, blocking Joey. "Not a chance, Escario—low man on the totem pole brings in the equipment."

Joey looked up at Nathan with more than agitation in his eyes. He was already anxious enough, but once again Nathan's condescension had managed to uproot a series of tangled emotions within him. His interior response never failed to remind Joey that his supposedly distant past was not so distant. He looked towards Jonathan for support but saw that he was already inside the music hall.

"Don't take it so bad, big guy. Maybe we'll get roadies one day." Nathan turned and scooted in through the back door, grinning to himself.

"Asshole," Joey mumbled just loud enough to be audible, yet low enough that Nathan would not hear him. He moved around towards the back of the truck to start unloading his equipment, but then stopped suddenly.

Two burly men were standing there with big, yet conspicuously phony grins on their faces. The darker-haired man spoke first.

"Tough having the most talent, yet the least say, isn't it, Joey?"

Joey looked at the two men suspiciously. "How do you know my name?"

The lighter-haired man responded this time. "Oh, we know lots about you, Joey, and even more about your talent. Please excuse me, I'm Bud and this is Nick." The man who identified himself as Bud paused momentarily. "You know, forgive me for saying this, but it's really too bad you got in with such a dead-end group."

Joey was still not buying it. "What do you guys want?"

"Well," Nick continued. "We are... *acquaintances* of a man by the name of Jimi T. Expo. Does that name sound familiar to you?"

"Sure, he's the guy Mr. LaVey's considering besides us."

Nick nodded. "Yes, that's partly true, Joey. Actually, he's pretty much already offered Mr. Expo the contract—save a soul-changing event taking place here tonight. We're here to ensure that won't happen."

Joey cocked his head with just a glint of understanding.

"So what are you here to do? Kick the shit out of me or something like that, so I can't play?"

The men exchanged glances, a smirk spreading across each of their faces. "No, Joey," the man identified as Bud responded. "We're not into that. We're here to make you an offer."

Joey looked suspiciously at the two. "What do you mean by 'an offer'?"

"What we mean is, we're giving you an opportunity to switch from being an over-talented artist in an ungrateful dead-end group to a respected musician with the most powerful performer of our time.

Joey did not respond immediately. "I was told that Jimi T. Expo played all of his own instruments, so I don't get where you're coming from."

Bud tried to mask his feelings of pleasure. They already had Joey, at the very least, allowing their offer to enter his mind. Bud continued. "That's true! Very true! But after the album is released, he'll need a band to back him up on the road. Mr. Expo is capable of many things, but playing the drums and guitar at the same time is not one of them."

Joey shifted his stance uncomfortably. "I-I've already got a band. I won't..."

"A band that values your talent? Be honest, Joey. Do you really think the way they treat you is going to change? Do you think that they're not going to pick up a new, *more experienced* drummer the first chance they get?"

Joey tried to hide the fact that he was struggling with what was being said. Nathan *was* very ungrateful towards him. Jon and Simon were all right, but they didn't always stick up for him when Nathan started in with his crap. Still, they had given him a shot. "I—"

"I'm not just here offering you empty promises, Joey. I'm prepared to front you a token of our goodwill in advance."

Nick reached into the inside of his coat pocket, pulling out a folded legal-sized envelope. He handed it to Joey.

"Go ahead and count it if you like. What you'll find is thirty one thousand-dollar bills. That's thirty thousand dollars upfront, and that's just the beginning."

Joey opened up the envelope and flipped through the money in utter amazement. He had never been so close to such a large sum of cash. He looked up at the two men, who were doing their very best to offer sincere smiles back to him. He glanced back at the envelope and his look of excitement faded. "What are you asking me to do?" he questioned noncommittally.

Bud spoke. "For right now, just let us go ahead and unload your equipment."

Joey looked up, confused. "Why do you want to do that?"

The two men exchanged serious glances. "I'm not going to lie to you, Joey, because you seem to be a very sharp young man. There is a price to pay for all of this. Even though Mr. Expo pretty much has the contract all tied up, we only like to deal in sure things. These talent agents, they get a bit emotional at live performances; it clouds their judgment and they make hasty, often bad decisions. Mr. Expo will obviously not have the opportunity to play for Mr. LaVey. So if Mr. LaVey has a few drinks, as he tends to do, and thinks he's really enjoyed the show, Mr. Expo may lose out on what is rightfully his. You know… music contracts aren't as plentiful as days of old."

Joey looked aimlessly back and forth between the two. "So you want me to play bad tonight?"

Nick looked stunned. "For the love of the Devil, no! We want you to shine out above the rest. It is the *others*—the ungrateful ones—that we prefer to have difficulties."

Bud jumped in. "That's right, Joey. We're just going to tamper with their equipment a bit, just to make up for the drunken earmuffs that LaVey's going to have on for tonight's show."

"You want to make us sound bad?"

"No, not bad. Just not quite up to par. It's really a small price to pay for what we are offering you. You guys will still have raised the money for your cause, people will still enjoy the night… and heck, you can even give some of your take there to the soup kitchen for all we care."

Joey stood motionless, trying to sort out all of this new information in his head. The money was nice, and playing for a true professional would be really neat. This deal would basically guarantee him of getting *something* out of tonight, no matter who was signed. And he *was* tired of being treated as a second-rate tag-along. Still...

...the guys had treated him better than anyone else had. Simon had let him stay at his place since they began. Jonathan always seemed to take the time to speak with him when he was down, and heck, Nathan did have his moments when he wasn't a complete asshole. It really did feel like magic playing with these guys, and he did not want to lose that feeling.

He mulled it over a moment longer, then slowly held out the envelope to the two men. "Sorry guys, I-I'm already in a band. Thanks for the offer though."

The two men glanced at each other, unable to conceal their disappointment. "Well, in that case, Joey, I'm afraid I'm going to have to give you this envelope instead."

The man called Nick pulled out a larger yellow envelope and handed it to Joey.

Joey took the envelope with a perplexed look on his face.

"Go ahead and open it, Tiger," the man called Nick stated with a smirk on his face.

Joey opened the envelope and immediately became aware that it was full of pictures. He pulled the first one out, and his face dropped.

Bud smiled, but Nick displayed a sarcastic note of concern. "Yes, Joey-boy, Bud here is quite the cameraman. I'd say he caught your good side in these shots. The other boy isn't quite as photogenic as you though, wouldn't you agree?"

Tears began to drip from Joey's eyes as he went through the pictures, slowly shaking his head.

Nick continued. "Yeah, I think it would definitely be a downer on your career after your adoring public saw these photos. Sure, we are a more tolerant nation, but still. You know, some of these positions I didn't think were physically possible... *especially with another boy!*" Nick whispered the final phrase of his comment with a sinister flair.

Joey shook his head as the tears were now streaming down his face. "No... please... things are different for me now. I've changed... please don't..."

Nick smiled, savoring each moment of the sadistic turn the conversation had taken. "So what's it going to be, Joey-boy? Envelope number one, or envelope number two?"

25

I have yet to uncover
The mystery
Of the elusive entity
Known as Night.

That stream of moments
Where dreams quietly infringe
On the edges of reality.

No thought is safe
From the night
No soul is fearless
Once forced to confront
The absence of clarity.

In the Night
I sense the extremes
    One moment
        A calming serenity
    Yet in the next
        A terrifying glimpse
        Into the endless abyss.

The Night holds the answers
To mankind's darkest secrets
    Whispering quietly
    A poor man's gossip
    To those feigning sleep
Feigning life.

DOMINION

The Night exists
For those who crave the vast unknown
Never discriminating
The rich from the poor
But catering
To each soul's dreams
And each man's fears.

The Night had been tapping at my window
But I do not hear Him now
Though I can do without His morbid thoughts
I must admit
My tortured conscience
Will certainly miss
His soothing indulgences
To my own transgressions.

– Jonathan Corban Storm
Night

i

"We've got a problem!" Clarence Hoover yelled out as he burst into Jake Hanssen's office.

Hanssen was on the phone, but after one glance at Hoover, he gave a quick, "I'll get back with you," and hung it up.

Hoover appeared excited, but a second look revealed a look of trepidation in his eyes. "We've got to go now! He's found the Freeman boy—I think. He's—"

Hanssen frowned, waving his hands. "Slow down, Hoover, no need to—"

"We've got to get there now!" Hoover interjected. "We just learned that Alexandre Nesterov landed at Wilmington International Airport and is on his way towards Pergamum with a bunch of men. Turns out the Freeman kid is playing at some kind of benefit concert there tonight. Nesterov must have found out about it and plans to off him there."

Hanssen's eyes widened. "What time does the concert start?"

"Eight o'clock, but Nesterov may not wait to enjoy the show."

Hanssen looked at his watch. It read six-seventeen. "Son of a bitch!" He yelled as he rose from his seat.

"Hoover, I want all operatives within a hundred-kilometer radius to drop everything and head for that location. I'll get the jet ready to fly us there immediately. Inform Edgar and tell him that the first man to spot the Freeman boy needs to grab him and get him out of there."

"Sir?" Hoover eyed him cautiously. "You want us to intervene without his permission?"

"I don't give a shit about permission! Nesterov's obviously found him, and if the Freeman boy gets whacked, the Witness Protection Program has lost every ounce of credibility it ever had. So stop standing there like a damn potted plant and get moving!"

ii

Jonathan, Nathan, and Simon stood on the stage, looking out in awe across the multitude of empty seats. They would be filled this night. Jonathan maintained his dreamy look. Nathan appeared to be tickled pink.

"This is awesome!" he shrieked.

A voice echoed out from somewhere offstage. "And it's only the beginning, boys."

The three looked around, confused at where the echoing voice had come from. They watched as a figure emerged from one of the last rows, walking down the aisle towards them.

The man who approached them was near two meters tall, yet weighing in at no more than eighty kilograms. His black hair hung well below shoulder level, and he had multiple earrings adorning each ear. Additional piercings and tattoos ornamented much of his visible flesh. His look was one of sheer intensity, but the smile he wore suggested a calm sense of self-confidence.

The three did not speak as the man hopped up on the stage.

"Hey there, men. Good to meet you." He reached out for Jonathan's hand. "My name is Esau LaVey."

A chill went through Jonathan's body as he shook the man's hand. Their eyes met, and Jonathan could have sworn he heard a burst of laughter inside his head.

Nathan, realizing that Jonathan was not going to immediately respond, took Mr. LaVey's hand. "Hello Mr. LaVey, I'm Nathan... Nathan Page. Please don't mind Jon here, he didn't sleep much last night, with the excitement and all."

LaVey nodded his head and finally broke Jonathan's stare. "Yes, I see."

Simon jumped in on cue. "Simon Wilson, sir. Pleased to meet you."

LaVey shook Simon's hand and then stepped back. "Well, don't let me stop you guys. I know you have a lot to do. I've got the contracts with me, and I hope when all the dust settles tonight, we'll be in business together."

"We look forward to it!" Nathan responded as LaVey turned away from them. Nathan could not help but notice the final glance he gave Jonathan before leaving.

He patted Jonathan on the back. "Don't go schizo on us now, Jon-boy, we need you tonight."

Jonathan nodded his head, still looking at LaVey as he walked off. He turned his gaze to Nathan, slightly glassy-eyed, then attempted a weak smile. "Sure, Nate, no problem. Let's go find the sound man."

They turned just as Joey walked in. He had almost half of his drum set in his hands. Simon and Nathan walked past him, Nathan messing up his hair and saying "Jooooo*eeeey*!"

Jonathan started to walk after Nathan, but paused when he realized Joey appeared to be avoiding eye contact.

"You okay, big man?" he asked.

"Sure, fine," Joey blurted out as he continued to move on.

Jonathan hesitated for a moment, then moved to follow the others backstage when he heard a familiar voice call his name.

"Jonathan!"

He turned to see his Aunt Vanya standing half inside the rear door of the hall, waving to him. He smiled and bounced back to see her. As he approached, she stepped fully inside the building. Jonathan watched as the next figure stepped in.

Jonathan stopped in his tracks, still ten meters away, when he saw his grandfather. Nesterov smiled and held his hand out to Jonathan, moving towards him.

"Good to see you, boy!" he called out, as Jonathan mechanically raised his hand for a shake. He shot a quick, agitated look at his aunt as she apprehensively approached the two.

"What are you doing here?" he asked, trying his best to sound polite.

Nesterov opened his mouth to answer, but Vanya jumped in. "I thought it would be nice for your grandparents to see how wonderfully you and your friends played."

"Grand*parents?*"

Just then Annie D. stepped in, and Jonathan's eyes lit up as he immediately moved to embrace her.

"God's good!" she whispered as she held her grandson tightly. "Please God, and the angels and saints for that matter, you'll be safe and sound. I'm so proud of you, Jesse."

Jonathan stepped back, unable to prevent tears from filling his eyes. Yet his joy was cut short as he glanced behind them and noticed a number of men in suits enter the building. He pursed his lips and looked down. "Just a regular family reunion, huh?"

Annie D. spoke up. "They'll never be family, Jesse. Not even a wee bit." Then looking the other way down the hall she said, "Well, I'll be back in two ticks. I've to run to the lav!"

Jonathan looked back at his grandfather, realizing that he needed to ease the atmosphere a bit. "Umm, well, Grandfather, I do want to thank you for making this possible."

Nesterov looked at him, obviously oblivious to what he meant. Jonathan picked up on it immediately.

"You know, getting us that gig with the recording studio."

Nesterov still looked perplexed. "Recording studio? Jonathan, I do not know of what you are speaking..."

Nathan realized Jonathan had not followed them out, so he turned and retraced his steps, re-emerging on the stage. He spotted Jonathan halfway back in the aisles and quickly recognized Mrs. Storm. Someone else was also with them, but his back was to him. Nathan smiled and hopped off the stage, moving towards them.

"Hey, Jon-boy," he called out in a friendly tone. "This is no time to be—"

His last word got stuck in his throat as the man speaking with the pair turned around. It was Alexandre Nesterov. All three smiled at him, but Nathan froze. He watched as Nesterov's expression switched from a congenial smile to one of mild confusion. Nathan instinctively turned, moving away quickly.

"Well, what in the world has gotten into Nathan?" Vanya asked curiously.

For a brief moment Jonathan glanced at his grandfather, who was still staring as if he had seen something familiar. Jonathan looked back towards the retreating Nathan, gave a polite, "I've gotta go," and then slipped away.

"Who was that boy, Vanya?" Nesterov inquired. "He looks familiar."

"Oh, that's Nathan Page. A dear boy. He was such a help when Jonny was ill, he..."

Vanya continued on, but Nesterov had tuned her out, trying desperately to figure out why the name 'Nathan' seemed to ring a bell with him. He was about to shrug it off when suddenly something clicked in his mind.

Jonathan tracked Nathan down in the backstage dressing room. When he walked in, he realized Nathan was trembling.

"Get away from me!" Nathan shrieked as he backed into the corner.

Jonathan was perplexed. "Nate, what's going on?"

"DON'T PLAY DAMNED STUPID WITH ME!" Nathan screamed in hysteria. "You and your mother work for Alexandre Nesterov. If that's even your mother at all!"

Jonathan's expression dropped at hearing his grandfather's name.

Nathan saw the transformation. "Yes, that's right, Jonathan, or whoever the hell you are." hot tears now burned down Nathan's face. "I know your game. I don't know why you waited so long to finish me off, but you're going to have a hell of a fight on your hands, you lying son of a bitch!"

Jonathan's mind was reeling. "Nate, why would I want to—?"

"Are you going to deny that you're in with Nesterov?" Nathan screamed.

Jonathan looked away, stepped back towards a nearby chair, and slumped down into it. He inhaled deeply, and then let out his long, heavy breath. He felt the protective walls which he had built over the years slowly start to crumble.

What's the use?

"He's my grandfather," Jonathan mumbled, barely louder than a whisper.

Nathan was about to yell again, but caught himself, finally absorbing the ramifications of what Jonathan had just said. He blurted out, half unsure of himself. "You're lying."

Jonathan looked up to him with an expression of shame. "Listen, Nathan, you've known me too long. You know I've never lied to you. I'm ashamed of my grandfather. I..." He paused for a moment, wondering if he should say what he was feeling. He shook his head. "No, no, that's not exactly true. I've allowed you to believe that Vanya is my real mother. She's not. She's my aunt. My real mother died giving birth to me."

Nathan allowed himself to take in everything Jonathan was saying through a sieve of skepticism. It was too much all at once. He shook his head as he sniffled back his tears. "No... it can't... why..."

Jonathan peered intently at Nathan. "Why would my grandfather want to kill you anyhow?"

Nathan looked carefully into Jonathan's eyes. He had nothing left. His parents were dead, he had been discovered, and now he was most likely not going to live to see another day. The only thing that still meant anything to him was the music. Jonathan had been his friend for too long, and if he couldn't believe in him either, well, then it was probably time to pack it in. He had nothing more to lose.

"My real name is Nathan *Freeman*," he began as a painful look of realization slowly came across Jonathan's face.

iii

Luther, traveling incognito in his blue jeans, black shirt, and not-too-subtle fedora cap, entered the theater at a separate gate from the rest of the crowd. Flashing his press pass, the security guard did not question him as he walked in.

The guard had been given a description of a very dangerous religious fanatic who might try to slip into the theater tonight, but what his eyes saw walk by him was a quite attractive young lady with press credentials.

The guard stepped back as the light rain turned into a downpour. A bolt of lightning flashed, and for just an instant, he could have sworn he saw two men in the rain, standing no more than thirty meters away. A second bolt lit the sky, and there was nothing. He pulled his glasses off, wiped them, then looked again. Still nothing. The security guard shook his head and diverted his attention to the next V.I.P. to come his way.

Luther walked through the back halls and ascended the stairs until he reached the room which had been prepared for him. He stepped in and moved forward to the glass of the viewing box, which looked down upon the stage where his son would be performing.

"Father."

The voice from behind him admittedly startled him. Luther spun around with a momentary ray of hope within him, yet his slight smile dropped when he saw Samuel Hagarot standing in the doorway.

The expression was not lost on Samuel, though Luther quickly recaptured a countenance that beamed approval.

"Good evening, my son. It is good for us to be here."

Samuel did not know exactly how to respond and looked downward, somewhat awkwardly.

"It has come to my attention that you have been quite busy," Luther breathed. "Busy with many, quite intriguing, activities."

Samuel looked up, a renewed sense of possibilities welling within him.

"Yes... I have been overseeing all. I must admit, I am quite proud of your accomplishments, and truly, today is to be a big day for you, and it is only the beginning…"

Samuel's eyes showed a flicker of life. In some ways, it disgusted him how much he desired this man's affirmation. Yet still, this was how it was to be, how it *should* be. Tonight, he clearly sensed it, was the night where his standing with his father would be made manifest.

Luther smiled and beckoned to Samuel to join him at the window box. He scanned the stage for Jesse, but without any luck. But no matter, the moment would come soon enough.

"I want you to see, my son. I want you to see what happens to one who has fallen into displeasure with me."

26

"The destruction of your bodies then will be the starting point for a rebirth, and their dissolution, a renewal of your former happiness. But your minds will be blinded, so that you will think the contrary, and will regard the punishment (life in the body) as a boon, and the change to a better state as a degradation and an outrage. But the more righteous among you... look forward to the change."

– Hermes

i

Alexandre Nesterov pulled Andrey Gavrilenkov aside, handing him the picture of Nathan Freeman which he had kept in his wallet.

"You and all the boys have this, right?" he asked.

"Sure... Freeman's kid."

"Right," Nesterov responded, looking over his shoulder to make sure that they were still out of earshot of Vanya.

"Listen, Andrey, the kid is here, he is playing tonight in the band."

Gavrilenkov was perplexed. "I thought this was your grandson's band. How is it that—?"

"The gods are smiling on us today, my friend. Alert the other boys... I will find Felix myself. I want the kid taken out, but *after* the show. Are we in good understanding?"

Gavrilenkov fought a momentary sense of queasiness. In all his years, he had never been involved in a hit on one so young. "Yes, sir. And what of this

Luther character?"

"Truth be known, my daughter sometimes has an active imagination. I have not heard a thing from anyone at the doors Still, do not be slack. I have a feeling this is going to be one hell of a night."

ii

As the theater began to reach capacity, Jonathan, Nathan, and now Joey sat silently in the dressing room. Simon entered, still maintaining his previously acquired emotional high.

"Dudes, the place is packed!" he announced happily.

In the next moment Simon became aware of the sullen faces on the rest of his band mates' faces.

"Ahh… okay… what gives, guys?"

Jonathan looked up, providing a somewhat strained smile. "Guess the situation's just a bit overwhelming. We'll get it together."

"I sure hope so," Simon responded. "Dude says we got five minutes till stage call."

Nathan and Joey looked up instinctively. A slight burst of adrenaline entered into their veins as their previous distractions began to fade. Jonathan looked at the others intently. A comforting smile began to emerge from his face.

"This is it, guys. This is what we were born for."

In any other context, Jonathan's statement would have seemed absurd. But part of each of them felt a certain truth to what he said. This had come together so quickly and so perfectly. The chemistry when they played together was indescribable. Yet no one could question that *it* was there; flowing, breathing, and at times wrestling within an unknown battle as it coalesced into something that transcended the temporal and reached into eternity.

"Two minutes to stage time," the voice called over the monitor.

"Let's do it," Nathan remarked.

The four moved slowly through the door toward the stage entrance. Yet just as they reached the stage door, something in the corner of the hallway caught Jonathan's eye. He paused momentarily, his ears not registering the

"Hey, Jon!" which echoed from Nathan's mouth.

A step closer and Jonathan's curious suspicions were confirmed. Here, backstage at the Rhine, was an old, beat-up harpsichord. The keys were cracked with sharp edges. Still, it had a piece of familiarity.

Jonathan stepped up to the instrument and ran his hands along it, caressing it as an old feeling of sadness swept over him. His hand slid down the left side when it hit something…

…an indentation.

His eyes widened as he bent down towards the side to see what he now knew to be there.

It was his and Tobias' carved-in names.

"Jon, what the hell? They're going to call us!"

The voice came from Nathan, who had walked up behind him.

"This is it," Jonathan responded dreamily. His misspelling of his brother's name in the carving confirmed that this was genuine. "It's Nanny Vanya's harpsichord. I don't know how, but it's—"

"Jon please… *please* don't be weird now." Nathan was on the verge of pleading. "Yeah, it's an old harpsichord, but that don't mean a thing. Besides, all the keys have sharp edges. You'd split your hands wide open."

Jonathan still did not move.

The loudspeaker cracked, as the M.C. thanked the crowd for their attendance towards such a worthy cause.

"Jon!" Now Nathan *was* pleading. "We need you. The band needs you!"

Jonathan looked towards Nathan, who now had Simon and Joey on either side.

"SO MAY I NOW INTRODUCE TO YOU, THE BOYS WHO MADE IT ALL POSSIBLE. LADIES AND GENTLEMEN, I GIVE YOU, THE PHOENIX!"

The crowd roared, and a glint of exhilaration sparked in Jonathan's eye. Nathan caught it and produced his own smile, this one of relief.

Jonathan felt his heart begin to race as he moved towards the stage entrance. The others followed, entering onto the still-darkened stage.

This is it, Jonathan reflected.

PHOENIX

Yes… that it is, a strangely familiar voice echoed out in his head.

He approached the microphone as Simon hit and sustained one resounding note on his synthesizer. It was so low it shook the house, along with the innards of every soul in attendance.

The cheers grew as the multicolored stage lights began to rise on the band.

In a world and a time marked by the loss of any cultural and spiritual identity, *The Phoenix* had emerged.

iii

Jake Hanssen and Clarence Hoover exited the jet and were immediately greeted by another agent, who shook their hands and led them to their car.

"Brian Silvis, sir. I work with Agent Edgar. We have seven men at your immediate disposal, with another fourteen for back up expected to arrive in the next two hours. What orders do you wish me to relay, sir?"

Hanssen and Silvis slipped into the back of the car, while Hoover hopped in front.

"Tell the men that they are to shoot Nesterov on sight."

Silvis could not restrain the look of shock which emerged from his face as the car began to move. "Sir?"

"You heard me," Hanssen responded, looking intently out the window of the vehicle. "Nesterov made headlines making asses out of us. Now we're going to make headlines saving the life of one of our operatives while unfortunately ending the life of a scum-sucking pig."

Silvis hesitated, still dumfounded.

"I MEAN NOW, SILVIS!"

27

The stage is set
The moment nears,
When darkness vents
Its reign of fear.

A distant self
Dissolved in shame,
Now grasps the One's
Unholy game.

With joy, embraced
A tainted dawn,
As Seraphs dance
The band plays on...

– Jimi T. Expo
Evolution

i

And the band played on...

The delicate, yet soul-piercing sounds which emanated from the stage could no longer be described as great chemistry. This was pure alchemy.

The crowd sat, mesmerized, as the members of *The Phoenix* allowed the sum of their entire lives to flow through them in the form of song. All of their prior troubles had passed like a dream, and they now realized they had not been born until this very night, baptized in a spirit not of this world.

Jonathan captured the souls of those present, carrying a stage presence with him that was unparalleled. The entire band sensed the company of something greater than themselves at work here. It was as if the secret language of music had been discovered, and a mystical truth not previously known had begun to peek out from its hidden abode.

No one was more astonished than Joey. After their second selection, he had become aware that whatever tampering those thugs had attempted to do with the equipment had failed. *The Phoenix* could not have sounded better.

Vanya and her parents sat mystified. Tears freely flowed from her eyes as she saw the boy who had lived such a troubled life finally break free from the fetters which had bound him. She sensed the peace in him. Alexandre too was moved. Somewhere, in the midst of the music, he had forgotten his purpose for attending. It was only Annie D. who sensed something slightly unsettling, like an unheard counter-melody. She dismissed the feeling, however, chalking it up to her close proximity to the man for whom her revulsion grew daily—the man to whom she was bound by Sacrament.

One in attendance did not share the goodwill felt by the others. Luther had to leave the original room he had been in and then gently *persuade* a security guard to allow him access to another box overlooking the stage, this one soundproof. Still, as he watched without sound, Luther could not diminish this mind-splitting headache that he had acquired while in the previous box. He had sent Samuel down to mingle amidst the throng, having given him a very specific assignment. Seeking to soothe his mind and body, Luther held his head while quietly chanting to himself.

A moment later he looked up in painful agony, and in his mind, uttered one word.

Now!

A thousand kilometers away, as Father Daniel Ananias attempted to extinguish the Easter Candle near the altar, it suddenly exploded in flame, splattering his face and body in hot wax. His eyes burned as he instinctively fell to his knees.

"Now!" he heard from within him. *"He needs your prayers, now…"*

As Jonathan led *The Phoenix* into its final barrage of sound, bringing to consummation what would be an unforgettable night, something slipped in his mind. A sudden feeling of vertigo nearly overcame him.

He looked up as the final note echoed off, followed by a spontaneous burst of applause. He felt a peculiar tingling sensation spread throughout his body as he looked to his right.

There, on the very edge of the stage, stood the harpsichord.

Nathan still had his arms raised in jubilation when he caught sight of Jonathan wandering off towards the right part of the stage. A second glance made him aware of what Jonathan was moving towards.

Cut the lights! he thought beyond all reasonable hope. It was clear Jonathan was zoning out again. Nathan turned his head as he went to place his guitar down when he was greeted with an eerie sound.

Silence.

He looked up to see the alarmed expressions on Simon and Joey's faces. In another instant, he heard a note played on the harpsichord. It was soon followed by another... and then another...

Jonathan felt the life force flow through him, passing through his fingers into the harpsichord. It was different somehow. It was struggling, yet he continued to play. The harpsichord gently reverberated throughout the auditorium. The tempo of this musical piece of unknown origin began to pick up more and more quickly. He burst into a crescendo when...

Suddenly, his fingers stopped. Feeling himself spiraling into a deeper and deeper trance, Jonathan slowly lifted his hands. His mouth opened as he saw the blood freely flowing from his sliced up palms.

He began to back away from the harpsichord, quickly being overcome by a paralyzing sense of terror. Sensing the deafening silence that surrounded him, Jonathan looked from his hands over towards Nathan.

Nathan stared back, unable to get his body to respond.

The fears which had gripped Joey prior to the concert had returned with a sweeping vengeance. In the instant after Jonathan had stopped playing, Joey's eyes had caught a dim, yet still visible light which began to blink from the public address system converter connecting the patch chord leading to

PHOENIX

Jonathan's microphone.

As he witnessed Jonathan move back towards center stage and raise his bloodied hand towards the microphone, the trance which held the entire auditorium snapped within Joey's mind. He screamed.

"NOOOOOOOOOOOOOOOOOOOOOOOOOOOOO!"

"God help us…" a terrified Vanya whispered.

Nathan's neck jerked in the direction of Joey. Absorbing Joey's expression in an instant, he shot his head back towards Jonathan as he watched his friend touch the microphone.

"JONNY!"

A bluish light seemed to emanate from the area where Jonathan stood as Nathan swore he could hear the sound of gunfire. A bright flash temporarily blinded him, and he felt himself falling.

The last image ingrained on Nathan's retinas before his world went dark was that of his best friend, Jonathan Corban Storm, engulfed in flames.

Citations

Chap	Reference
	Andersen, Hans Christian. *The Phoenix Bird* (1850)
1	Eliot, Thomas Stearns. *The Hollow Men, Poems: 1909-1925*, T.S. Eliot, 1925.
4	Herrick, Robert. (1591-1674)
5	Wangerin, Walter, Jr. *The Book of Sorrows*, Zondervan, 1996.
6	Heraclitus. (ca 500 B.C.)
8	Durrell, Lawrence. (1912-1990)
10	Gauntlet, Lori.
11	Aesop. *The Blind Man and the Whelp*, (ca 620—560 B.C.)
13	Alighieri, Dante. (1265-1321) *Inferno* (IX-6:45), ca 1307.
14	Cousins, Norman. (1915-1990).
19	Eckhart, Meister. (1260-1328).
20	Wangerin, Walter, Jr. *The Book of Sorrows*, Zondervan, 1996.
21	Wordsworth, William. (1770-1850).
22	Spinoza, Benedict. (1632-1677) *Ethics, Part IV, Preface*, (1677).
23	Mechthild of Magdeburg. (1210—ca 1285/1291).
26	Hermes

For additional information on authors, artists, works, and quotes cited in *Dominion* (including the ability to purchase) please visit www.thedominionproject.com/citations.html

The Dominion Project continues with Book III

TRYST

Beckoning Fate

Following the calamitous debut of *The Phoenix*, a traumatized Simon and grief-stricken Nathan reunite in an attempt to pull the pieces back together. With the fate of Jonathan shrouded in mystery, a new figure is emerging on the world scene—the enigmatic musician/philosopher Jimi T. Expo. His music takes the world by storm, and its accompanying quasi-religious movement, *The Way of Mystic Realism*, seems to spread like wildfire, filling the deepest yearnings of each soul who dares to embrace it. In the eye of the storm, Nathan and Simon struggle to navigate the transforming landscape of this new world, drawn irresistibly towards an unknown destination—and an un-chosen fate.

Order your copy at

www.thedominionproject.com

Direct Ordering of the Dominion Series

Especially for those who do not have online access, all books can be purchased direct from T.C.C./Sacrata Dei Press by mail.

Dominion – The Series

Book I: Seed   *(June 2009)*
Book II: Phoenix   *(July 2009)*
Book III: Tryst   *(August 2009)*
Book VI: Requiem   *(October 2009)*
Book V: Ascension   *(December 2009)*
Book VI: Abyss   *(May 2010)*
Book VII: Revelation   *(January 2011)*

Dominion – Reference

For the Dominion reading enthusiast who wishes to delve deeper into the series, these brief reader's companions/reference are a helpful tool providing character profiles, time and location references, summaries, background, and descriptions. Each Interlude is meant to follow its corresponding book from the series, offering a more in-depth understanding of the "Dominion world" while further preparing the reader for the next book.

First Interlude
Second Interlude
Third Interlude
Fourth Interlude
Fifth Interlude
Sixth Interlude
Coda: Deux Ex Machina

Please call (574) 307-0413 for current mailing address, shipping rates, and tax rates (where applicable). Once obtained, please identify in your mailing your name and address, which book(s) you are ordering and the quantity, and provide a check or money order in U.S. dollars made payable to T.C.C./Sacrata Dei Press.

www.ingramcontent.com/pod-product-compliance
Lightning Source LLC
Chambersburg PA
CBHW020603250626
47154CB00004B/1339